ARTFUL ANTICS AT ST BRIDE'S

DEBBIE YOUNG

Boldwood

First published in Great Britain in 2023 by Boldwood Books Ltd.

Copyright © Debbie Young, 2023

Cover Design by Rachel Lawston

Cover Illustration: Rachel Lawston

A CIP catalogue record for this book is available from the British Library.

Paperback ISBN 978-1-80483-137-3

Large Print ISBN 978-1-80483-136-6

Hardback ISBN 978-1-80483-138-0

Ebook ISBN 978-1-80483-135-9

Kindle ISBN 978-1-80483-133-5

Audio CD ISBN 978-1-80483-143-4

MP3 CD ISBN 978-1-80483-142-7

Digital audio download ISBN 978-1-80483-140-3

Boldwood Books Ltd
23 Bowerdean Street
London SW6 3TN
www.boldwoodbooks.com

Dedicated to the memory of my late German teacher, Frau Rosemarie Nunn, who taught me so much more than German.

'A girl might do anything she aspires to do, if she is sufficiently determined.'

> — GEMMA LAMB – ST BRIDES SCHOOL FOR GIRLS

'You should always trust a man,' observed Sapt, fitting the key in the lock, 'just as far as you can.'

> — ANTHONY HOPE – THE PRISONER OF ZENDA

1

FRESH START, DAMP SQUIB

The familiar clunk of the chunky Victorian key turning in the lock of the door to my school flat made me smile in anticipation of the familiar violet vista within. Picking up a travelling bag in each hand, I shouldered the door open and raised my right elbow to flick on the light switch.

One glance within made me gasp. I looked back at the sign on the door. Had I got the wrong flat? No, the engraved brass plaque said 'Lavender' – but the colour scheme was more suggestive of the girls' nickname for it: the Lavatory. The resplendent purple carpet and curtains around the big bay window had morphed into a muddy brown.

Suddenly, a flurry of tiny sparks flew out of the light switch, crackling, before the chandelier sputtered and went out. The darkness rendered the soft furnishings even murkier.

I dropped my bags in the corridor and left the door wide open to allow light to spill into my flat, which lay in darkness as I'd left the curtains closed when I left for the half-term holiday. As I crossed the room to open them, the carpet squelched beneath my feet. After the first few steps, I walked on tiptoe to diminish the revolting sound. My stomach churned.

The floor-length curtains were now so weighty with water that I needed both hands to draw them back. As I tugged on the cold, wet cloth, thick, grimy liquid trickled down my wrists and inside my coat sleeves, making me shudder.

A cracking sound above my head made me look up, just in time to see damp shards of plaster detaching themselves from the ornate cornice and tumble to the floor. Too late, I realised my mouth was open, and I shut it quick, before spitting out several greying fragments of ornate plaster that reminded me of wedding cake icing decades past its best.

A creak and a rustle alerted me to the fact that the left-hand end of the curtain rail was starting to come away from its fixings, the disintegrating plaster no longer strong enough to bear its weight.

My gaze travelled across the ceiling. Once a creamy white, the matt surface was now mottled with brown cracks, each adorned with a row of tiny drips, stalactites in the making as the plaster liquefied.

I covered my eyes in horror until a volley of raps on the still-open front door made me spin round to see who it was. Oriana, elegant as ever in a daffodil-yellow jersey shift dress and crocus-orange stilettos, was standing on the threshold, her arms folded tightly across her chest. She'd chosen a light-brown colour for her hair to start the term, and her new graduated bob, longer at the front than at the back, was gleaming with health – or at least with the application of some effective products. Her perfect make-up echoed the colour scheme of her outfit. Not many women could have carried off her bright-orange lipstick and yellow eyeshadow. It was far from my taste – I stick to natural-look cosmetics and have never coloured my hair – and my wardrobe of year-round neutral separates pales against her fashion choices.

'Your flat too, then?' she asked, her tone sympathetic for once. 'Mine's like a flipping sauna, only without the heat. Water's running down the walls, and half my kitchenette ceiling has collapsed. We can't sleep here tonight. Let's go and gang up on the bursar and make him sort out alternative accommodation for us pronto. Come on, before the girls get back and distract him with their nonsense.'

I squelched my way back to the door across the waterlogged carpet and closed the door behind me.

'I haven't got as far as checking my kitchenette,' I said, 'but perhaps I'd better avoid it until I can be sure the ceiling isn't going to come down on my head.'

As I brushed my hands over my hair, scraps of damp plaster rained down on my shoulders.

Oriana began to stride ahead in the direction of the bursar's office.

'My wallpaper's peeling off,' she said tersely. 'Those old banknotes I'd stuck on my walls are turning into papier mâché on my carpet.'

I took a couple of extra steps to keep up with her.

'I blame it on the roof,' she continued. 'The bursar's been whining on for years about the fragility of the tiles over this part of the building. This'll teach him to neglect it. Now, instead of just fixing the roof, he'll have to redecorate our entire flats.'

I felt a little sorry for the bursar, who struggled to run the school's vast estate on a shoestring. The maintenance costs ate up a substantial chunk of the pupils' fees. Even so, I was glad to have the formidable Oriana as an ally in this disaster. She'd never take 'no' for an answer. Together, we'd get a better and faster resolution than if I had to tackle the bursar on my own, plus she held the ace card of kinship. The bursar was her biological father, a fact she and her half-brother Oliver had only discovered the previous term, although he knew all along. No doubt he'd do whatever it took to keep her on side.

When we arrived outside the bursar's office, Oriana hammered on the door with the insistence of a bailiff. His reply of 'Enter' sounded slightly startled, and no wonder. This stage of the term, before the girls returned en masse, should have been calm for him, albeit the calm before the storm.

When Oriana opened the door, the bursar smiled in relief to see it was only us. He may have presumed our visit was a social call, just to say hello after the half-term break, but his smile quickly faded when he saw Oriana's angry expression and my plaster-speckled hair.

'Hello, Oriana, Gemma,' he began carefully. 'Am I to judge from your faces that you are less than happy to be back at work?'

With uncharacteristic inelegance, Oriana slumped into one of the visitors' chairs in front of his desk. Perhaps she felt she could let down her guard a little now that she knew he was her father.

'It's that damned roof you're always complaining about, Bursar,' she declared. I'd been wondering what name she'd decided to call him since the familial revelations that had emerged before half-term. She'd always known that Hairnet – Miss Harnett, the headmistress – was her mother, but the official story was that the former head of governors, the late Piers Galsworthy, who died not long after her birth, was her father. But before Hairnet had begun her fling with Mr Galsworthy, she'd already conceived Oriana from her longstanding affair with the bursar, which came to an abrupt end when her mother discovered the bursar had fathered a son, Oliver, with the wife of Galsworthy; Galsworthy himself was actually infertile.

When I came to work at a girls' boarding school, I never expected such complicated relationships between staff, but now they seemed the norm.

Anyway, it seemed Oriana had decided to keep things formal with the bursar, as she did with her mother, the headmistress, at least when on duty. 'I've been telling you for years about the drips from my bathroom ceiling. Whatever weakness in the roof was causing that leak must have spread out across the whole roof of our wing because my flat and Gemma's are now absolutely sodden. We can't possibly live there until the roof has been fixed and the flats completely refurbished. It's an utter mess.'

I held up my grimy hands in evidence.

'And if you don't get the roof fixed fast,' she went on, 'it's only going to get worse.'

The bursar clapped a hand to his forehead and grimaced.

'Oh, no! That's going to cost us a pretty penny. A pretty penny not currently in our coffers. Especially at this time of the school year. The next school fees aren't due for two months.'

He ran his fingers through his hair in a gesture of mild desperation. 'Everything here is Grade I listed, you know, Gemma. It's not like getting your roof fixed at home. English Heritage insists on appropriate materials, the replacement of like with like.'

I was glad about that. Every detail of this beautiful house had been carefully specified by its original owner, the wealthy Victorian gentleman Lord Bunting, working in tandem with the best architects of his day. It would be tragic – although undeniably cheaper – if repairs were made using substandard materials, replacing the slate roof tiles with imitation, or patching up the fine Bath stone with concrete and cement. The handmade silk wallcoverings in a single room might cost more than the average decorating budget for an entire family home, but it would be tragic to replace its sheen with factory-made wallpaper from a DIY superstore.

As he scraped back his chair and got to his feet, he picked up a clipboard from his desk. 'Still, if it's as bad as you say, it'll have to be done. I'd better go and take a look.' He sighed. 'I'm beginning to wish we'd never taken that break abroad over half-term, Oriana. Then I'd have been here to address the leak as it happened and nip it in the bud. I hear the rain was torrential in this part of the Cotswolds while we were away.'

'Leaks,' hissed Oriana to emphasise the scale of the problem.

I turned to Oriana as she rose from her chair.

'You were away over half-term?'

When she tossed her head, her hair bounced so healthily that it reminded me of a hairspray advert.

'Yes. My mother insisted on us playing happy families for a change.'

Her tone was cynical, but the way she avoided eye contact suggested to me that this arrangement had meant more to her than she wanted to let on. After being raised by a single parent, she had found herself part of a classical family unit, with mother, father, son and daughter. I hoped their holiday had been a happy one, for all their sakes.

'Did you go somewhere nice?' I asked, hoping to elicit some details. Usually, she and Hairnet spent their holidays at the school, the vast house and gardens providing a lavish private home in the absence of the staff and girls. The change of scene should have done them both good. I'd spent the half-term break partly with my parents and partly with Joe at a little hotel on the Dorset coast.

'Madeira,' she replied. That explained her light tan. Knowing Oriana's affinity for make-up, I'd assumed her healthy glow had come out of a bottle. 'The bursar got a cheap, last-minute deal after the end of term for a five-day break. He has his uses.'

Coming from Oriana, that was praise indeed.

As we left, the bursar, with old-fashioned courtesy, rushed out from behind his desk to hold the door open for us.

'Actually, it was gorgeous. The perfect climate, and not at all busy. We had a very nice time getting to know each other better, just the four of us.'

As we approached the stairs, she gave me a quick glance as if to anticipate my reaction before she spoke. 'Oliver came too.' I was glad about that. I liked her half-brother, the bursar's son. I knew nothing about his mother, the late Mrs Galsworthy, who had raised him as her husband's child, but it seemed to me that she'd done a good job with him, and not just because she was very wealthy, having inherited her late husband's fortune.

'It seems a long time ago now though,' she added as we turned into the corridor containing our staff flats.

Oriana unlocked her front door and flung it open to show him the extent of the damage.

'I should imagine the cost of the holiday would be a drop in the ocean compared to what this little lot will cost,' he said with a heavy sigh. 'And of course, you can't possibly live here until it's fixed. I'll speak to the housekeeper to see what else is available.'

'Gerry will be up to his ears preparing the dorms for the girls' return,' replied Oriana. She glanced at her watch. 'Leave it to us. We'll go up now to the old servants' quarters and scout around for suitable rooms to tide us over.'

'The old butler's flat will do for one of you,' said the bursar. He had lived there himself for a few difficult weeks in the autumn term. He didn't sound exactly enraptured at the memory. 'There's another flat of similar size beside it, opposite Joe's. They'll be unlocked just now, but Gerry will be able to give you the keys for whichever you choose.'

I lowered my eyes so as not to betray my delight at the prospect of living closer to Joe, even if we obeyed the school rule about staff keeping out of each other's flats.

'Meanwhile, I'll go and alert Miss Harnett to the issue and we can put our heads together about financial solutions.'

He did not sound hopeful.

As he trudged off in the direction of the headmistress's study, head bowed, we scooped up our bags and headed for the stairs to the attic, feeling like refugees.

2

PETTY PROBLEMS

Oriana took what had once been Lord Bunting's butler's flat, and I took what the former head housemaid's room opposite Joe's. Neither were en suite, unlike our staff flats, but it seemed they were the best we were going to get.

We just had time to transfer to them whatever possessions we could salvage from our flats before grabbing a quick coffee in the staffroom to fortify us for the girls' arrival and our official return to duty.

A week away from Old Faithful, the school coffee machine, had given me just enough time to break my termtime caffeine addiction. Forgetting the scalding temperature maintained by the little hotplate beneath the pot, I burned my tongue with the first sip, then winced at the rich, dark taste. Topping my cup up with milk to cool and dilute it softened the blow psychologically, even though I knew I'd still take on board the same amount of caffeine, just in a paler, less painful form.

A rapid series of taps sounded at the staffroom door. I set down my coffee without finishing it and swung the door open just enough to see who had knocked without allowing the pupils to glimpse the hallowed secrets of the staffroom.

'Hello, girls, welcome back.'

They tried to peer in anyway, jostling against each other to peep past me. I leaned against the edge of the door to block as much of their view as I could.

'Hello, Miss Lamb, same to you. Please may we tell you our exciting idea for the new term?'

I was tempted to suggest they save it until teatime, when we'd all be sitting comfortably around the dining room table and would have more leisure to chat, but they looked as if they might burst with excitement if they didn't let their idea out soon.

'Okay, but make it quick, please. I've a cup of coffee getting cold in here.' As I spoke, I realised those few sips had reignited my addiction.

'Well,' said Imogen, putting her hands on her hips, 'my friends and I have just been thinking how lovely it would be if we could bring our pets to school with us. We're missing them already.'

I'd shed a secret tear at leaving my mum and dad's new kitten at the end of my latest visit, so I wasn't without sympathy.

'I can understand that you might have felt sad saying goodbye to them before you came back to school, but I'm not sure bringing them with you would be very practical.'

'Oh, but we'd look after them ourselves, miss. It wouldn't make any work for you or the other teachers. We'd feed them and brush them and take them for walks.'

'The ones with legs, anyway,' put in Rosalie. 'My tropical fish don't need to go for walks.'

'My snake's got no legs, but I could still take it for walks to be sociable,' said Zara brightly. 'My gran's always saying how good it is for you to have a change of scene.'

I shuddered.

'Anyway, you're busy all day with lessons and prep and activities and Essential Skills training,' I countered. 'You wouldn't have time to look after your pets properly too.'

'Other schools let their pupils bring pets,' objected Rosalie, twiddling a loose strand of white-blonde hair around her index finger. 'Why can't St Bride's?'

Imogen wriggled her way to the front of the group and raised an instructional forefinger. The others took a step back to allow her to make what seemed likely to be a carefully planned and rehearsed statement.

'My next-door-neighbour at home, Amaryllis, says that at her school, the girls are allowed to take their ponies with them. They compete at local gymkhanas and Pony Club events for the honour of their school. So they're actually helping the school by taking their ponies with them.'

I suppressed a smile.

'Perhaps Amaryllis's school is a different kind to ours. One with stables, for a start. St Bride's doesn't have any stables.'

That wasn't strictly true, but what had once been a courtyard full of stables was now our teaching area, with the stalls converted into classrooms.

'They must have bigger desks, too,' observed Ayesha, twisting her dark waist-length plait between her fingers. 'A pony would never get its legs under our desks.'

'They don't take their ponies into lessons, silly,' said Rosalie, her baby-blue eyes crinkling in laughter. 'The girls go to see them after lessons in their stables. Amaryllis's mother says it teaches the girls to be responsible.'

The mere thought of the costs of stabling the horses would have sent the bursar into a tailspin of anxiety. I did my best to extinguish this suggestion before it became a rumour, only to disappoint the girls when it turned out to be false.

'In any case, perhaps it's better to keep your pets at home so they don't distract you. Then you can look forward to being reunited with them at the end of term.'

'If they're still alive,' said Ayesha, knitting her silky dark brows.

The girls' faces fell.

I was about to retort that they didn't think that way about their parents, but I stopped myself just in time. The school had been set up to educate motherless girls, and although some of our pupils had acquired stepmothers, they'd all lost their biological mothers. I tried a different tack.

'Think how sad it would make your fathers to be without your pets all term, as well as missing you. It's all right for you girls – you've got lots of human friends here for company.'

'My dad would only have my little brother otherwise.' Angela's tone indicated she thought that a raw deal.

Perhaps I was starting to turn the tide of their opinion.

'Besides, we've got our lovely school pet, McPhee, for you to share,' I added.

Right on cue, Miss Harnett's large, black cat came padding silently towards the staffroom. When I pointed at him, the girls turned round, crying, 'Aw!' and 'Ah!' before piling in to stroke him. McPhee's tolerance was admirable. He sat down to accept their pats and strokes with good grace. I could hear his appreciative purring above their assorted shrieks.

McPhee had an uncanny ability to know when a child – or indeed an adult – was particularly in need of his attentions. I was pleased to see he was on form for the start of term. After a moment, he stretched his front paws out in front of him then arched his back.

'Oh look, McPhee's doing yoga!' said Isobel. 'Do you think we could teach him to do more tricks?'

Before they could try, he turned his back on them and paced sedately along the corridor to where Hairnet was welcoming a new pupil. The tall, slender girl of indeterminate age was dressed in a puff-sleeved, white blouse under a forest-green, dirndl-skirted pinafore dress that reached her knees. Two thick, tight, white-blonde plaits, which started high above her ears, hung heavily down her back. When McPhee reached the girl, he weaved around her ankles, rubbing his chin against her long, white ankle socks. Her patent black Mary-Jane shoes were as black and glossy as his fur.

The girl pressed her hands to her cheeks in horror. 'Go away, cat!' She stretched up on tiptoes, as if trying to remove as much of herself as possible from the creature's reach. If she'd had levitational powers, I think she'd have used them.

The posse of girls who had been talking to me ran after McPhee to defend his honour.

'Don't speak to McPhee like that,' cried Imogen. 'You'll hurt his feelings. McPhee is our school pet. You have to be kind to him.'

Hairnet peered at them over her glasses.

'My dears, not everyone in the world is as fond of cats as we are. People who have never had the chance to get to know a cat before may need a little time to grow to love dear McPhee.'

The new girl wrapped her arms around herself defensively.

'I will never learn to love a cat. I hate cats. They were cruel to my *Kanarien*.' As she spoke, I detected a German accent. 'A black cat killed one of my *Kanarien* when a bad man set them free.'

Ayesha bent down to give McPhee a reassuring stroke, running her small, slender hand from the top of his head to the tip of his tail.

'I expect it was just doing what cats do,' she said in his defence. 'It was just being a cat. Anyway, you shouldn't take it out on McPhee. It wasn't him who killed your whatever it was.'

'McPhee chases the squirrels and rabbits in the grounds here,' said Imogen. 'But I've never seen him catch a *Kanarien*.'

'What's a *Kanarien* anyway?' asked Rosalie. 'Do we have them in England?'

'It's German for canaries,' I told them. I'd learned a little German in my own schooldays. 'You know, those little yellow birds. Like a budgie, only smaller. People used to keep canaries as pets because of their song. Not so much now, as many pet owners don't hold with keeping birds in captivity these days.'

'Only the man bird sing,' said the new girl. 'But their song is very beautiful.'

Hairnet laid a comforting hand on the girl's shoulder.

'Perhaps your little birds are happier in the wild,' she said gently. 'Let us picture your canaries singing happy songs fluttering about the beautiful trees of your homeland.'

The girl shrugged, and Hairnet withdrew her hand.

'Now, please excuse me, girls, but I must introduce Frieda to Miss Taylor, who is to be her housemistress.' Hairnet wiggled her fingers at the younger girls as an instruction to disperse. 'Run along and unpack, and it will be teatime before you know it.'

'Yes, Miss Harnett,' they chorused.

'Bye, Frieda,' said Imogen pleasantly, apparently holding no grudge against the new girl's hostility, and remembering her manners. 'And welcome to St Bride's, by the way.'

Her friends echoed her words, but Frieda's face remained sullen.

'*You're* welcome to St Bride's,' she replied stonily.

But when she thought no one was looking, I saw her bite back a smile.

3

A GIRL CALLED PEACE

Hairnet turned to me.

'Miss Lamb, might you be so kind as to take care of Frieda while I fetch Miss Taylor from the staffroom?'

Although I could almost hear my cup of coffee calling me from the staffroom, there was only one acceptable answer.

For a moment, I wondered why Hairnet hadn't asked one of the girls to fetch her, then I guessed she wanted to brief Hazel about our new pupil out of the girl's earshot. There might have been sensitive issues in her background best discussed in private.

I led Frieda to the plump Chesterfield sofa in the entrance hall to await Hairnet's return with Hazel. McPhee followed her, eyeing her lap in hope of an invitation, but she crossed her legs away from him. Taking the hint, he slunk off towards the library, where he might have expected a more appreciative reception from returning pupils in whose eyes he could do no wrong.

'I'm sorry about your canaries,' I began, attempting to be conciliatory. 'What a sad thing to happen.'

Her face contorted with grief, although I noticed her eyes remained dry.

'I am sad too. I will never see them again. Nor my mother. She is dead too.'

How odd to mention her canaries before her mother, I thought. Perhaps she found it harder to talk about the far greater tragedy. Odd not to shed even the tiniest tear, though, no matter how brave a front she might be trying to present, but everyone grieves in their own way.

'I'm so sorry for your loss,' I began. 'But I hope you will find comfort in befriending other girls at St Bride's who have sadly also lost their mothers. They will understand from their own experience a little of what you are going through.'

She shrugged. '*Vielleicht.*' Maybe…

Her composure made her seem very mature compared to some of the other girls, who cried buckets at the slightest loss, such as losing a favourite pen.

I was struggling to identify her accent. She was clearly a German speaker, but her accent was not quite like any I'd heard when I'd visited Germany as a schoolgirl on an exchange programme. Perhaps she was from another German-speaking country, such as Austria, or Switzerland? I remembered my own high school German teacher trying to persuade me to study the language to GCSE because of how widely it was spoken beyond Germany. Belgium and Luxembourg also counted German as one of their official languages. Perhaps Liechtenstein too? Although I was pretty sure there were still German-speaking enclaves in South America and Africa, Frieda's dress didn't suggest she'd come from warmer climates. Actually, it didn't even look as if it had come from the present day. Perhaps she was a time traveller, I mused, although I knew this couldn't be true.

'Your homeland,' I began, curious for the answer, but she cut me off.

'I do not speak of my homeland.' She clapped her hands

together hard, as if to symbolise the finality of her decision. 'It is dead to me. As dead as my mother.'

I scrabbled to lift the mood.

'Miss Taylor is our head of art as well as the sixth form housemistress. Do you enjoy art?'

Frieda put her head on one side, rather bird-like herself for a moment.

'I think you want me to say yes.'

The distinctive sound of Hairnet's brogues was approaching from the staffroom, accompanied by the gentle squeak of the canvas, rubber-soled shoes favoured by Hazel Taylor, Head of art. I leapt to my feet, eager to hand Frieda over.

'Here's your housemistress to welcome you now,' I declared, with a wave of my hand. 'Miss Taylor, meet Frieda – Frieda...?'

I realised I didn't know her surname. The girl helped me out.

'Ehrlich. *Ich heisse Fräulein Frieda Ehrlich.*' She got to her feet, gave a little bow, and clicked the heels of her shiny Mary Janes together. 'My name means peace. Truly, peace.'

'Ah, as in Krieg und Frieden,' I observed. 'The German title for Tolstoy's *War and Peace*. And you are right, Ehrlich means truly.'

She narrowed her dark, deep-set eyes at me. 'Do you think I do not know the meaning of my own name?'

Hazel's straight, fine eyebrows shot up in surprise at the girl's rudeness. Doubtless she didn't want to scold Frieda when she'd only just arrived, but, not usually one to tolerate rudeness, she'd tell me in the staffroom later what she wished she could have said to put the child in her place.

I was glad Frieda was going to be in Hazel's house rather than mine. Firm but kind, Hazel would not stand for any nonsense.

To be fair, the girl looked a little shocked herself at her own display of cheek. I wondered whether her brusque manner was a front to hide her nervousness. It wasn't that long since I was a new girl at St Bride's myself – well, a new member of staff, anyway. I could remember feeling intimidated initially by this huge, grand building. Perhaps she did too.

'Well, I'm glad to know the meaning of your name too.' The ever-generous Hazel gave a kindly smile that Frieda did not return. 'I'm afraid I don't speak German, so I wouldn't have known. I'm also interested to hear that Miss Harnett has awarded you an art scholarship in recognition of your talent.'

Hazel must have been surprised that Hairnet had offered our new pupil this special status without consulting her. To be honest, Frieda looked rather startled about it herself, a flush coming to her pale cheek as Hazel congratulated her. Perhaps she suspected she didn't deserve it, but had been given it out of pity for her plight. It wouldn't be the first time that the kind-hearted Hairnet had given a special award to a new pupil to lift her spirits and build her self-esteem as she joined the school. Poor Frieda did look as she could do with a boost after all she had been through. I hoped she'd start to feel more cheerful once she'd made a few friends among her peer group.

I was glad she had come for selfish reasons too. The school didn't usually acquire new pupils in the middle of the school year, so whatever her father was paying in fees would be a bonus to the school budget. I hoped it might be enough to cover the roof repairs and the redecoration of my flat and Oriana's.

More footsteps echoed from along the corridor, this time the distinctive plod of the bursar's stout shoes, plus an unfamiliar but distinctly male step from the direction of his office. A moment later the bursar came into view, accompanied by a tall, dark-haired, male visitor in a forest-green, collarless, woollen jacked and dark-grey flannel trousers. The visitor smiled encouragingly at the frowning Frieda.

Hazel stepped forward, holding out her hand for the stranger to shake. 'Ah, you must be Herr Ehrlich.'

For a moment, Frieda looked as if she was going to laugh at Hazel's assumption, then she covered her mouth with her hand and coughed, as if pulling herself together.

'Sebastian Goldman-Coutts,' replied the stranger, in deep, clipped, velvety tones. He straightened his back, planted his feet close together, and for a moment I thought he was about to salute. Not that his dress was military, but the knife-sharp crease in his grey trousers and the gleam of his black lace-ups made me wonder whether he'd spent any time in the armed forces. 'I am Frieda's sponsor and a near neighbour of the school. I live – we live – at Torrid Manor, a couple of miles this side of Tetbury.'

Unlike Frieda, he spoke perfect King's English that gave me no clue to his origins, other than suggesting he'd had an expensive private education. Eton, Oxford, then Sandhurst, perhaps?

'Are you also her guardian?' I queried. '*In loco parentis*?'

'Ah no, she has no need of a guardian,' he replied, clasping his hands behind his back and parting his shiny shoes slightly, as if his superior had just barked, '*Stand at ease!*' I forced myself to concentrate on his reply. 'Her father, Herr Ehrlich, is in my employ. I have just appointed him as my assistant, and it is my pleasure to sponsor his daughter's education at St Bride's as part of his remuneration.'

'Frieda tilted her head on one side and gave him a quizzical look.

'An assistant who must drive your car and dig your garden.'

'A very valuable assistant to me in more ways than one,' said Mr Goldman-Coutts smoothly, locking eyes with her.

The corners of his lips twitched as if they were sharing some kind of private joke, though I failed to see the funny side. If I were Frieda, I'd have shown a little more courtesy in the face of such generosity. St Bride's annual fees were surely higher than a gardener's annual wages. Mr Goldman-Coutts must have been a very rich benefactor as well as a generous one.

His name certainly sounded like money. It put me in mind of *The Great Gatsby*, which I was about to start studying with the Year 12s. '*Her voice is full of money*,' says Gatsby of Daisy Buchanan.

I was surprised Hairnet had granted Frieda an art scholarship if she had such a wealthy sponsor. He sounded as if he could afford the full fees. Maybe she wanted to butter him up, hoping to encourage him to sponsor further girls in need, or to endow a new facility for the school, such as a theatre.

Mr Goldman-Coutts smiled warmly at the girl.

'Now, Frieda, if you are ready to settle in, you may go out to my car to say goodbye to your father.' He turned to Hazel. 'Please excuse him for not coming in. He is waiting in my car. Herr Ehrlich is rather a shy man.'

I wondered whether he might also be depressed, still grieving for his late wife, or perhaps he was just embarrassed by his lowly position and having to rely on someone else's charity to pay his daughter's school fees.

Frieda did not hesitate, striding to the door with a strength and energy that belied her willowy form, her legs slender inside those neat, white socks. As soon as she had left the building, Miss Taylor addressed Mr Goldman-Coutts.

'Miss Harnett has just been filling me in on the sad circumstances of Frieda's background. But please do not worry. We will soon have her feeling right at home at St Bride's. As an art scholar, she will have my special attention to draw out her talent.'

Mr Goldman-Coutts' dark eyes twinkled.

'No pun intended?'

Hazel grinned. 'No. But more seriously, I sincerely hope and believe that she'll find her art a great therapy and comfort as she processes her bereavement. It will also provide an excellent nonverbal arena in which she may shine, independent of her grasp of the English language. And if you would ever like a tour of my art studio, you have only to ask.'

Suddenly the art scholarship made sense. Hazel had been badgering the bursar for a new art studio, to replace the current one in the long attic space above the academic classrooms.

Mr Goldman-Coutts gave a slight bow.

'Miss Taylor, you are too kind.'

'As indeed are you.'

Feeling superfluous, I bade him farewell and returned to the staffroom, where the remains of my coffee were stone cold.

4

THE ELUSIVE TYCOON

'I can't help wondering what's in it for Mr Moneybags,' said Mavis Brook next morning as we sat at the staffroom table writing in our daily planners. I'd been telling her about my encounter with Frieda and her sponsor. Head of geography and school librarian, Mavis had been at the school much longer than me; I thought she might have known more about our near neighbour.

She swapped her blue pen for a red one.

'Nope. Not a sausage. But why hasn't Hairnet tried to involve him in school life before? Or to tap him for funds if he's so filthy rich? I would if I were her.'

St Bride's run by Mavis would be a very different place.

After a quick scribble on the page, she closed her planner with a snap.

'She could at least invite him to join the board of governors, if only to reduce the average age,' I mused. 'Mind you, we'd have to wait a long time for a legacy in his will. I'd put him in his late thirties.'

'And yet the girl's gone into the sixth form?' asked Mavis. 'He must have started young. But hang on, Mr Moneybags is only her sponsor, isn't he? Her father could be any age.'

I hesitated. 'Actually, I'm not sure how old her father is, nor Frieda. Hairnet's put her in Year 12, but the way she dresses makes her look a lot younger. Like she's stepped straight out of Mayenfeld, with her Alpine gear and her long, blonde plaits.'

'Mayenfeld?' She gazed into space, as if trying to place it on the map: a geography teacher's natural first reaction. Then she realised why the name sounded familiar. 'Oh, you mean where Heidi lives in the old Johanna Spyri novel? I suppose she might be from the German-speaking part of Switzerland.'

'She does have an unusual accent, as far as my schoolgirl German can tell.'

Mavis nodded. 'I don't speak it myself, but I do know the Swiss version of German, *Schweitzerdeutsch*, is quite different from the German spoken in Germany, which of course also has lots of regional accents of its own, just like English in England.'

'Wherever she's from, you'd think a girl of sixth-form age would dress in a more adult fashion. Those long, white socks and demure skirt are very childish.'

Mavis chewed the end of her red pen. 'Sounds like she's fresh from the Chalet School.'

Oriana came to lean against the edge of our table.

'You don't usually hear of people leaving Switzerland voluntarily. Quite the opposite. People clamour to get in. Well, rich people, anyway.'

Her eyes glazed over at the thought.

Mavis closed the exercise book she'd been marking.

'Maybe she's not Swiss. It's very hard to get Swiss citizenship.'

Oriana patted her smooth, dark bob.

'I'll ask the bursar later. He'll know her nationality because her father will have had to put it on her registration form.'

'Oh, but her father didn't register her,' I explained. 'He stayed in the car all the time she was here.'

'All on his own?' asked Mavis. 'How very anti-social.'

'Maybe that's where she gets her attitude from,' I mused.

'Oh, I don't know,' said Joe from his usual armchair. 'I saw Max chatting to him, keeping him company. They seemed to be getting along just fine. Max was keeping him entertained.'

Mavis raised an eyebrow.

'Max Security? That man of few words? He's hardly a cabaret act.'

'Anyway,' I continued, 'it was her sponsor who did the necessary with the bursar.'

'Sponsor?' Joe looked up from his newspaper.

'Well, he described himself as her sponsor. He's footing the bill for her fees, anyway.'

Oriana gave a huff of indignation. 'You mean the German fellow driving that Rolls-Royce was only the chauffeur? I saw him out there when I was saying goodbye to Tanya's father and I thought he was the new girl's father. He didn't look like a chauffeur. He had much more class. And earlier, when I saw Hairnet talking to him on the forecourt, she all but dropped a curtsey to him.'

Hairnet's curtsey reflex in the presence of a title was legendary. She was no snob, and refused to use the girls' titles in school, but she knew her etiquette.

'No, you misread him, I'm afraid,' I told her. 'He's a chauffeur all right, and a gardener too. While you were busy eyeing up the chauffeur, Oriana, his employer was inside talking to Hazel and me. One Sebastian Goldman-Coutts in case you're wondering.'

'Posh bloke who lives at Torrid Manor, apparently,' added Mavis. 'You're slipping if he wasn't on your radar.'

Oriana folded her arms.

'What, his name's Coutts, as in the banking dynasty? Bank brand for HNWIs?'

'High net worth individuals,' translated Joe for anyone who moved in less privileged circles.

'Well, one of you might have told me. Why has she or the bursar never invited him to the school before?'

'My sentiments exactly,' murmured Mavis. 'Maybe he's a fraud. I mean, if you wanted to dream up a name that made the bearer sound rich, you couldn't do much better than Sebastian Goldman-Coutts, short of adding an extra surname and making it triple-barrelled: the ultimate status symbol for the overprivileged.'

'Presumably he has no motherless daughters of his own to send here,' said Joe, practically.

'Does he have a childless wife?' asked Oriana in a careless tone that fooled none of us.

Joe rolled his eyes.

'Here she goes again. "It is a truth universally acknowledged…"'

Joe had been reading *Pride and Prejudice* during half-term, trying to impress upon me that PE teachers read books too. Lately we'd got into an agreeably cosy habit of drinking cocoa and reading together in the library at the end of our day's duties. At least, that gave us a respectable excuse to spend our leisure time in each other's company every evening, once the girls were all in bed, although I confess, we didn't always get much reading done.

Mavis sniggered, but Oriana perked up. 'Yes, I think I could live with a name like that. Let me just Google Earth Torrid Manor on my phone. I've only seen the sign on the wall as I've driven past. You can't see the house at all from the road. The boundary walls and gates are quite overgrown. I suppose he must be into conservation. There's probably a stunning wildlife garden tucked away in there.'

She strolled over to the window seat for a stronger mobile phone signal.

'And after that, I'll Google his name to see what he's worth overall.'

I laughed.

'Oriana, you are incorrigible.' I teased her.

Mavis drained her cup of coffee and nodded at mine.

'Sup up, Miss Lamb, Hairnet will be here any minute for the staff meeting, and you know she doesn't like us drinking while she's speaking to us.'

I finished my coffee and returned our empty cups to the trolley just as Hairnet entered the staffroom, followed by the bursar, clipboard in hand.

5

ESSENTIAL BUSINESS

Hairnet didn't spend long on the start-of-term formalities to welcome us back before launching into the topic that was clearly front of mind for her and the bursar: raising money to repair the roof. Further investigation by the bursar had revealed leaks in several other rooms on the same wing as my flat and Oriana's. Fortunately, the other rooms were unoccupied, used only for the storage of rarely used materials and equipment, such as Christmas decorations and the Speech Day marquee, but the repair job was even bigger than he'd anticipated.

'So we're calling this term's Essential Skills Challenge, "Raise the Roof with Your New Business",' Hairnet announced, making eye contact with each of the teachers in turn as if to ensure our cooperation. 'As you know, several girls are already running successful businesses in their own modest – and safe – way, trading in home-made jewellery and handicrafts via Itsy Bitsy.' I assumed she meant Etsy. Modern technology wasn't her strong point. 'Those girls can be mentors and role models for the others, in whatever line of business they choose. Although the purpose of these new businesses will be rather different: we will launch the programme with an inspirational and informative talk by someone seasoned in managing a successful business and who has much wisdom to share.'

The bursar seemed to grow a few centimetres taller at this remark, only to shrink back at her next statement.

'A couple of you have already met Mr Goldman-Coutts, the generous sponsor of our delightful new sixth form pupil, Frieda Ehrlich.'

Hazel and I exchanged glances. Even though, like me, she always tried to see the best in our girls, I don't think either of us would have applied the adjective 'delightful' to Frieda.

'The rest of you will soon have the opportunity to meet the dear man. He has kindly agreed to address the girls after lunch tomorrow, despite his busy schedule.'

Mavis raised her hand. 'Miss Harnett, just what is Mr Goldman-Coutts' line of business that qualifies him to advise a hundred adolescent girls?'

Oriana raised a well-manicured forefinger, as if too indolent to put up her whole hand.

'Whatever it is, it's making him extremely rich. I looked up his estate on Google Earth and it's massive. Torrid Manor's a huge mansion, with countless outhouses, far more than a home of that size might need for stables or coach houses or garden bothies. He must be fabulously good at whatever his line of business is.'

'Torrid Manor?' Judith raised an eyebrow. 'I didn't think anyone had lived there for years.'

'Nonsense,' retorted Oriana. 'He told Hazel and Gemma that's where he lives.'

Silenced by Oriana's curt manner, Judith pressed her lips together. I suspected Judith knew more than she was letting on. I decided to have a quiet word with her as soon as I could get her on her own. She had been a wise and supportive friend to me, and I trusted her judgement more than Oriana's.

'It doesn't follow,' said Mavis. 'He might have inherited a huge property portfolio from his father and be in the process of squandering it on decadent living and business ineptitude. I'm sure we can all think of figures in public life with a similar record.'

'Actual wealth trumps earning power in my book,' retorted Oriana. 'Provided a man's rich enough for life, I don't care whether or not he's an entrepreneurial genius. What matters is the here and now.'

Hairnet clapped her hands as if bringing bickering pupils to order. 'Girls, girls! Please! Mr Goldman-Coutts' family background is irrelevant to the matter in hand. In any case, Oriana, I can tell you that he has neither wife nor children. You can be sure I queried the possibility of him sending his own daughters to us when his assistant, Herr Ehrlich, approached me about sponsoring Frieda just before the half-term break.'

'So what is his line of business?' Mavis repeated, never easily put off her stride. It was a reasonable question, but Hairnet turned to the bursar for clarification.

'Import and export,' he replied crisply.

'That covers a multitude of sins,' observed Mavis. 'He could be like Del Boy in *Only Fools and Horses*.'

Hazel put up her hand.

'Miss Harnett, you said there's a significant difference between what our existing young entrepreneurs are doing and this new Essential Skills project. What is that difference, please?'

'The profit from the Essential Skills business projects will go towards the new roof fund,' Hairnet replied. 'For which we urgently need contributions.'

'You can say that again,' declared Oriana, looking at me as if for moral support.

Nicolette, the French teacher, was sitting furthest away from Hairnet on the window seat. She stood up to ask her question. 'I hope we will not exploit the girls?'

The bursar shook his head vigorously.

Methinks the bursar doth protest too much, I thought.

'Not at all,' Hairnet continued. 'This will be a wonderful opportunity for them to do voluntary work in aid of a good cause. Any girls whose business raises money for the good of the school will have her name engraved on a tile for the new roof and on a plaque on the wall, so her success will not go unrewarded. Plus of course she'll learn valuable new skills that will stand her in good stead for later in life. Besides, the exercise will also enable us to discuss ethical business principles that are kind to its employees, fair to its customers, and do not harm the environment. There will be a certificate at the end of term for all our young entrepreneurs, regardless of their profit or loss.'

'Well, let's hope for plenty of profit,' said Oriana. 'I want my flat back by the end of term, and in a fit state to withstand any April showers during the Easter holidays.'

'I think we all want that, my dear.' Hairnet's tone was soothing, but firm enough to indicate that she considered the discussion closed.

The shrill clang of the bell heralded the start of the first lesson, sparing Hairnet and the bursar from any further questions. We'd have to wait until morning break to speculate out of their hearing as to the true nature of Mr Goldman-Coutts' mysterious business.

6

IN THE NAME OF MONEY

'I do hope he's part of the Coutts private banking dynasty,' said Oriana as we headed for the staff noticeboard at break. 'They're as sound as a bank can be. I sneaked a look at their website during my last lesson, when the girls had their heads down solving quadratic equations. Coutts Bank has been around since the eighteenth century and their clientele includes royalty. I bet Sebastian hobnobs with all sorts of wealthy people.' She was the only member of staff who had used his first name so far, already assuming a certain intimacy. I had to admire her self-confidence, if not her motives. 'I expect he invites them to his country estate for house parties. I wonder whether he plays polo?'

Her imagination was clearly running wild at the thought of not only a billionaire bachelor on her doorstep, but one with a network of equally affluent and eligible clients, friends, and acquaintances.

In a rare act of consideration for others, she poured me a coffee before serving her own. As she drifted away to daydream in splendid isolation on the window seat, Judith came over to join me for a chat.

'Gemma, you saw this Goldman-Coutts fellow earlier, didn't you?'

I nodded, curious as to her take on him. Judith was shrewd as well as discreet, and I trusted her judgement. If she had formed views on our new pupil's sponsor, I'd want to hear them.

'Yes, he seemed a normal sort of guy. Well, NFSB, anyway.' That's Normal for St Bride's. 'Very posh. So precisely spoken that he was almost too precise, like a foreign spy trying to pass for an Englishman.'

Judith laughed.

'Maybe it was just the contrast with Frieda's odd accent that made him sound so correct,' she said. 'I had her in my history class just now and found her voice strangely compelling. The girl has a certain presence. Anyway, back to this posh bloke. Did you talk about his house at all?'

She was watching me carefully.

'No, not at all. But I wouldn't normally speak to a child's parent or guardian, or indeed sponsor, about his house. Where and how the pupils live when they're not at St Bride's is no business of mine, although it's always fun to pick up snippets of information eavesdropping on the girls' conversations. Did you know one of the Year 7s lives in a house with a minstrels' gallery? Anyway, why do you ask?'

'Because I know for a fact that no one has lived in Torrid Manor for years. It's as overgrown as Sleeping Beauty's castle.'

'Oriana's take on that is that he's a keen conservationist cultivating a wildlife garden.'

Judith, mid-sip, spluttered into her coffee. 'If she'd seen how derelict the house is, she'd soon change her mind.'

'How do you know about the house? It's not visible from the road.'

Judith looked round to check no one was listening.

'Since Christmas I've been dating a really lovely estate agent from Dixon and Son in Tetbury.'

I gasped, then clapped my hand over my mouth for fear of drawing attention to our little chat.

'You dark horse, Judith! But how lovely. I'm so pleased for you.'

It wasn't easy to find romance when working at a boarding school, and I was pleased Judith had met someone nice.

'Thanks, Gemma. But here's the thing: Roger took me to see the place when the previous owner asked him to sell it for him. Simon said then that anyone buying Torrid Manor at its current asking price would be mad.'

'Did he give Mr Goldman-Coutts a special deal because it was a fixer-upper?'

'Actually, Simon didn't sell it to him. He tried his best to find a buyer, but just couldn't shift it. He was open with enquirers that it would cost more than the asking price to make it habitable and take years of work.'

'Gosh, an honest estate agent! He sounds like a keeper!'

Judith grinned.

'Yes, and that's why he resigned the commission in the end. He feared a less scrupulous rival firm might offload it on some poor, ignorant townie kidding themselves they'd live like a lord of the manor in it.'

'Looks like he was right. Oh dear.'

We'd gravitated towards the staff noticeboard while we were talking, where Joe was standing, frowning. As we approached, he tapped his name on a printed list with his whistle.

'They've made me responsible for sponsorship.'

'Presumably because you used to attract big-name sponsorship during your sporting career?' I suggested.

'I suppose so. I just hope Hairnet isn't expecting me to get big-name brands to back whatever little businesses the kids come up with. I sometimes wonder whether Hairnet has any grasp of the real world beyond our boundary walls. Besides, that part of my life is over now. I've no desire to revisit it. I've moved on.' I could see that he must have been uncomfortable with having to try to monetise his sport, which he'd pursued for the love of it, rather than for financial gain. 'I can't help wishing she'd given me something a bit more intellectually stimulating. I may only be a PE teacher, but it doesn't mean I'm dim.'

Oriana strode over to see what the fuss was about.

'Oh, for goodness' sake, stop whining, Joe,' she said briskly. 'Get over yourself.'

Joe didn't rise to her bait.

'Persuasive writing for me,' I noted, trying to divert them from arguing. 'That's a relief. It's on my curriculum anyway for each year group at some point, so I can just rejig my year plan to bring it forward to this term.'

Oriana peered at the entry by her name. 'Accounts for me, jointly with the bursar. *Quelle surprise!* Why can't the bursar cover that topic on his own? He's a grown up, for goodness' sake. Lazy devil.'

Joe grinned. 'Pot, kettle, Miss Bliss.'

She gave him a token slap on the upper arm.

'There are so many more interesting ways I could help them, such as showing the girls how to dress for success. Top tips on how to turn out for an important presentation, for example.'

She had a point.

'You could always volunteer a coaching session on that too,' I said.

Secretly, I was glad that her accounting role might make her spend more quality time with the bursar. It would do them both good. I suspected they were more alike than she gave him credit for.

The rest of the allocated tasks made similar sense. As head of geography, Mavis was to advise on socio-economic and geographical targeting. I hoped this would enable her to direct the girls beyond the school community. Otherwise, as the only adults they would encounter during term-time, we were sitting ducks for their sales pitches.

Science teacher Dr Fleming, analytical and objective, would advise on quality control, while Judith, school archivist as well as head of history, would oversee their businesses' online presence. Most likely she'd focus on restricting it for safeguarding purposes, rather than trying to amplify their visibility.

As head of art, Hazel was happy with her assignment: to direct the design and presentation of marketing materials. I looked forward to working in partnership with her when our two areas of responsibility overlapped.

The upbeat and resourceful Felicity Button, who managed the Essential Skills programme each term, was to guide the girls in any event management associated with their businesses, such as a sale of work.

The gentle Nicolette Renoir, who taught French, got off relatively lightly, tasked only with helping the girls translate their marketing materials into her native tongue, the only other language beside English on the St Bride's curriculum.

With a last glance at the noticeboard, Joe and I made for the sofa to finish our coffee. We sat side-by-side, close enough for me to feel the warmth of his body emanating through his tracksuit. He leaned towards me and spoke in a low voice full of mischief.

'Old Oriana's losing her touch if she hasn't noticed a bachelor billionaire living close at hand.'

I grinned.

'Perhaps he's the reclusive type. After all, when you buy a walled estate in the middle of nowhere, you don't do it to throw yourself into community life. Or perhaps he spends most of his working week in the City being a banker and is hardly ever down this way.'

'If indeed he is a banker,' mused Joe. 'That's just Oriana's wishful thinking. The bursar said he's in import/export. I don't think dealing in money counts. Still, it does seem odd that Oriana didn't know anything about him until now.' When I turned to look at him, I couldn't help smiling.

'What puppy dog eyes! I reckon they're the real reason that Hairnet put you down for sponsorship. It's nothing to do with your former career. She must think that if you turn that doleful expression on the right target, you'll persuade anyone to stump up a bit of dosh to support our young entrepreneurs.'

Our conversation was cut short by Mavis lumbering towards us. She thumped the far arm of the sofa.

'Budge up, lovebirds.'

We did, willingly. It was no hardship to move closer together.

'My money's on Oriana inveigling herself an invitation to Goldman-Coutts Towers before he gets through his presentation tomorrow.'

Joe gave a wry smile. 'I'd be foolish to bet against that. And I'm curious to see how she'll do it.'

I was more curious to discover how much time Mr Goldman-Coutts spent at Torrid Manor, or whether his work – whatever that was, exactly – kept him in London or elsewhere, which might account for why no one at school had never heard of him before. Hairnet was usually very good at building close relationships with wealthy neighbours who she might mould into school benefactors. How had he escaped her radar until now?

7

MONKEY BUSINESS

The younger girls often disconcerted me with their uncanny mixture of innocence and worldly wisdom. Cleverly, they pivoted Hairnet's challenge into animal-centred enterprises as an alternative to bringing their own pets into school.

'I vote we offer a pet-care service for local people,' said Imogen as the youngest girls in my house, St Clare's, were settling into bed in their dormitory that night. 'You know, dog-grooming and stuff like that. People could bring us in their dogs when they get scruffy or muddy, and we can give them baths and haircuts and trim their nails.'

'I painted my dog's toenails pink over half-term, and they looked really pretty,' said Veronica. 'I could do that for other people's dogs. That could be one of our services.'

I tried to picture a dog's paw. 'Do dogs have toenails? Sorry, I'm more of a cat person.'

'Well, claws, then,' said Veronica. 'And while I'm painting a dog's claws, someone else could be removing its ticks and fleas. Dogs get a lot of ticks when they go out for walks in the country, not like in London where I live.'

I wasn't sure where the school's health and safety policy would stand on that score. We'd have to complete a risk assessment, but for child or dog? Probably both.

'So, what can we do for cats?' Cecilia piped up. 'I'm like you, Miss. I like cats more than dogs.'

'They don't like being taken for walks though,' said Veronica. 'Even when I put our dog's lead on our cat, Twiglet, she isn't keen. But cats do like to be nice and clean, so maybe we could offer a cat cleaning service, like a mini car wash. And for long-haired ones, we could style their fur – plait it, highlight it, that sort of thing.'

I tried to steer them onto a course of action that wouldn't require the mass import of other people's pets.

'How about making accessories for cats and dogs instead? Collars for dogs and cats, and coats or sweaters for the less furry kind of dog that needs extra warmth on winter walks. And for cats, you could stitch little toys filled with catnip.'

Imogen's smile faded. 'My dad says catnip is like a drug for cats. It makes our cat Toffee go bananas.'

'Then you should change his name to Banoffee, like the pie we had for pudding tonight!' Cecilia's quip sent all the girls into fits of giggles.

Once their laughter had died down, Angela put her hand up to speak. 'Perhaps we could breed pedigree dogs. My Auntie Katie breeds cockapoos, and it's flipping brilliant because she gets to have puppies in her house all the time. Then she sells them for lots of money and gets on with breeding some more.'

I diverted them from the horrors of the pedigree system by reminding them of the criteria for their Essential Skills businesses.

'Remember, you have less than two months to make your businesses a success, girls. I don't know what the gestation period is for puppies, but a scheme like that would take far too long.'

'Are you suggesting people eat our puppies?' cried Angela. 'I'm sure no one eats my Auntie Katie's cockapoos'.

'In France they eat horses,' put in Imogen in a helpful tone. 'Does your Auntie Katie sell any of her puppies to France?'

I held up my hands for silence.

'Girls, girls, no one is suggesting anyone eat puppies. I said gestation, not digestion. That's an entirely different matter. It's from the Latin *gestare*, which means "to give birth to". Digestion comes from *genere*, Latin for "to carry", with the prefix dis meaning "to separate" as in "dissect".'

The girls' eyes glazed over as my mini Latin lesson interrupted their creative flow. I made a mental note to suggest to Hairnet basic Latin be included in a future Essential Skills project. I'd always been glad that I'd studied it for a couple of years at school, as it helps you deduce the meaning of so many English words.

'What I mean is, girls, that if you started trying to breed a pair of dogs today, you'd be unable to sell any puppies for four or five months. Even if you're successful at the first attempt, it would take a couple of months for the puppies to be born, then it would some weeks before they'd be old enough to leave their mother. Besides, you can't just set yourself up as a pedigree dog breeder. You have to be a certified expert and meet stringent standards of hygiene and animal welfare.'

'Like my Auntie Katie does,' said Angela proudly.

Rosalie shrugged. 'I don't think it's as difficult as you're making it sound, Miss Lamb. My gran said her Jack Russell gets pregnant just by going for a walk in the park off her lead.'

Imogen's quick thinking spared me from pursuing that line of conversation.

'Maybe we could breed something that grows a bit quicker. Didn't Dr Fleming say in Biology last term that the smaller the animal, the shorter its lifecycle?'

All eyes turned in sympathy on Cecilia, the tiniest girl in the school. I rushed to reassure her that all people, no matter how tall or short, have the same average life expectancy.

'You know, Miss, elephants and blue whales take ages to have their babies,' said Zara. 'While mice pop out babies just about every day.'

'So let's try breeding mice,' suggested Ayesha. 'Small animals won't take up much room either, so they're easier all round.'

'But will people want to buy them?' enquired Zara. 'My uncle paid a firm to come in and take mice away from his house. He certainly wouldn't have paid to get more. The firm kept coming back to seal up all their holes until the mice just had to move out and find somewhere else to live, like *The Borrowers*.'

'I suppose if any mice didn't get out in time, they'd be walled up like nuns in the olden days,' added Imogen. 'Mrs Gosling was telling us about that in history. It was hideous.'

'Or rabbits,' said Angela. 'Rabbits are really easy to breed.'

'Yes, that's why there are so many in the school grounds,' said Ayesha. 'We've loads of rabbits.'

That was true. You could often spot little grey-brown bunnies grazing the school lawns when the gardeners weren't around to shoo them away.

'Perhaps we could catch them and sell them,' Ayesha added.

Angela wrinkled her nose, which for a moment I mistook for a rabbit impression.

'But they're like the opposite to pedigree dogs. They have no rarity value. We wouldn't get much money for something people can just help themselves to for free on a country walk. If they're quick enough, anyway. We'd be better off breeding rare, unusual animals.'

Imogen bounced on the edge of her bed.

'I know, we could cross McPhee with a squirrel to produce a cat that eats nuts. There must be lots of people who'd like to buy a vegetarian cat. We'd be like its inventors, then it would get named after us, like the King Charles Spaniel.'

'Did King Charles invent the spaniel?' Ayesha's mouth fell open in surprise. 'Gosh, he's done well. He hasn't even been king for very long.'

The other girls fell about laughing, as did I, before Ayesha realised her mistake.

'Oh, of course, he's the third English king called Charles, isn't he? It must have been one of his prequels. I wonder what they'll name after our King Charles? I think he likes dogs.'

'Perhaps we could set up a business to keep the King's dogs safe?' mused Imogen. 'You know, against kidnappers or thieves.'

This wasn't as outlandish a suggestion as it might seem. The King's country residence, Highgrove, lay in the same part of the Cotswolds as St Bride's. I wondered whether Mr Goldman-Coutts was part of the King's social circle. That might account for why the tycoon kept out of the public eye locally. If he was hobnobbing with the King, his special guest's privacy would have to come first.

'A good business needs more than one client,' counselled Veronica. 'My dad says it's bad practice to be too reliant on any single customer.'

'But we can't look after lots of people's pets all at once,' objected Isobel.

Actually you can't look after anybody's pets in school, I thought, but kept quiet, curious to see where this conversation might go if left unchecked.

'No, but we could just look after the lost ones,' declared Imogen. 'Or rather, look out for them. We'll be pet detectives. We'll set up a pet detective agency.'

She raised her arm in victory, like an athlete crossing the finishing line.

'If someone loses their cat or dog, they call us and we help find them. Then we look after the pets we find until we can reunite them with their owner and send them a bill for our fee.'

She plumped up her pillows and climbed into bed with the satisfied air of someone whose work is done.

Angela frowned. 'That's easy for you to say, but how do we do that? We're not allowed beyond the school grounds in term-time unless we're on an outing or going to a doctor's or dentist's appointment with a member of staff. It'd only work if the pets get lost in our school grounds.'

Imogen nestled back against her pillows and pulled her duvet up to her chest. The dormitory was not very warm. Although spring bulbs were coming up in the grounds now, indoors it still felt like winter.

'Well, that's the easy part, and this is why my scheme is so clever,' said Imogen. 'Do you know what my dad does when he loses his glasses or his keys or his mobile phone? Which he does all the time, by the way. He says a prayer to St Anthony. That's the patron saint of lost things. He always says it aloud, so everyone can hear it. And it works every time, because, do you know, within a few minutes, Amélie, our au pair, has found them for him.'

'So we can be like remote control detectives,' said Ayesha. 'We just need to know which pets have gone missing and we say a prayer on the owner's behalf until they turn up.'

'Get your pa to text that prayer to you, Immy,' said Veronica. 'Then we can start to use it right away. Now, it's time for our bedtime story, isn't it, Miss Lamb?'

The girls had now all settled into bed and were looking at me expectantly for the day's final act of community.

'Yes, new term, new book,' I said, running my eye over the old, oak bookshelf beside my armchair. 'I think this one would be just right.'

I selected a dark-green hardback with gilt lettering on the spine, opened it at the first page, and began to read.

'The First Chapter. Once upon a time, many years ago – when our grandfathers were little children – there was a doctor; and his name was Dolittle...'

8

THE TYCOON'S ADVICE

Hairnet had scheduled Mr Goldman-Coutts's inspirational talk for after lunch the following day. I was looking forward to seeing him in action and as a businessman, rather than in the guise of a pupil's sponsor.

At school assemblies, the girls sat on the parquet floor, worn smooth enough over the years to be free of splinters. The teachers sit on chairs dotted along either side of the assembly hall to keep an eye on the girls' behaviour. This arrangement meant staff could not speak or signal to each other, or even exchange knowing looks during the process. Now I think of it, perhaps another reason for this traditional seating plan was to keep the staff in order as much as the girls.

I usually sat halfway down the right-hand side of the hall, as close to Joe as possible, while Oriana favoured the chair at the back left-hand corner to allow for a speedy getaway. Today, however, she plumped for the one at the front left of the assembly hall, closest to Hairnet's lectern. Oriana's hair looked freshly brushed and hair-sprayed into submission. Although I couldn't see her face, I guessed she'd touched up her make-up too. Today's outfit was a case study in power dressing. Judging by the padded shoulders, her classic business skirt suit was possibly of 1980s vintage. Earlier, I'd noticed the pearl cluster brooch pinned just below the shoulder of her tailored jacket was in the same position favoured by the late Queen and Margaret Thatcher. Her long legs in sheer tights and gleaming black patent stilettos were demurely crossed at the ankles. Presumably her goal was to present her most immaculate, elegant self for the benefit of our guest speaker. But was it enough to reel him in for a date?

As Hairnet entered the hall, the girls stopped chattering, their respectful silence during assemblies a school custom. However, the entry of Mr Goldman-Coutts just behind Hairnet caused a ripple of speculative murmurs.

To my surprise, he was accompanied by Frieda's father, his chauffeur. Perhaps the kindly Hairnet had extended the invitation to Herr Ehrlich to give him the opportunity to observe his daughter during the course of a normal school day, perhaps in hope of demonstrating that she was settling in well. Although Frieda hadn't yet formed any close friendships among her peers – while not uncivil, she retained a formal, distant manner rather than actively seeking to build friendships – at least she was looking a little more comfortable than on her first day.

I sneaked a glance over my shoulder to gauge his daughter's reaction. I was pleased to see she was beaming at him proudly. It was refreshing to realise she didn't seem to feel any shame or embarrassment that her father's job was far humbler than those of her friends' fathers, who were mostly high up in industry or the arts, or just independently wealthy with no apparent need to work. It was heartening to observe the obvious warmth in her relationship with her father. His fond, affectionate smile faded only when his employer began speaking. Then his brow clouded, as if worried as to what Mr Goldman-Coutts might say.

As I turned to our esteemed speaker, who had also caught Frieda's eye and given her a friendly nod of recognition. Still acclimatising to the strange environment, Frieda must have been glad to see both her father and her sponsor in school.

My heart went out to Oriana when I saw how Mr Goldman-Coutts was dressed. He presented a completely different image to his business-like appearance when he first brought Frieda to St Bride's. Perhaps he no longer felt the need to make a good impression on Hairnet and the bursar, now that the child had been accepted as a pupil.

Beneath a battered, black, leather biker jacket, he wore an ageing once-white t-shirt, above scruffy, faded-blue jeans and camel-coloured, suede desert boots. His thick, straight, black hair touching his collar was so tousled that I was surprised Hairnet hadn't instructed him to comb it. Yet on his left little finger glinted a huge, gold signet ring, and as he turned back the cuffs of his jacket, the thick gold bracelet of a chunky watch glittered. It looked to me like one of those eye-wateringly expensive types featured in full-page colour ads in the Sunday supplements, with pictures of handsome fathers and spotless sons, pitching the watch as a family heirloom to be passed down generations. I wondered whether Mr Goldman-Coutts had had to buy his own. I was sitting too far from him to be able to identify its brand, but doubtless Oriana would tell at a glance and would share that knowledge in the staffroom later on.

But I was getting as bad as Oriana, I chided myself, focusing on the man's outward indicators of wealth rather than listening to what he had to say. The girls weren't the only ones who might learn something useful from him. I sat up straight and clasped my hands in my lap, determined to pay attention to whatever business wisdom and life hacks he had to impart.

When my head jerked back, to my embarrassment I realised I'd dozed off. The low, flat drone of our guest's deep voice as he had introduced himself, followed by a string of soulless platitudes had been a soporific combination. In my defence, I'd not been sleeping well in my uncomfortable temporary accommodation. I glanced across to Mavis, sitting across the hall from me, to see whether she'd noticed my little nap, but she was too busy cleaning her nails with the cap of a cheap ballpoint pen.

Although I could only see the back of Oriana's head, it was clear she was at least pretending to be transfixed by his address. Opposite her, Hazel Taylor, a fixed smile on her face, was nodding now and again. Was she really agreeing with what he was saying? 'Early to bed, early to rise' was his current theme. Or was she just trying to win his favour – and his investment in her art studio – by being an appreciative audience? Oops, no, her eyes had closed. She was napping too.

And little wonder. Everything he was saying could have been lifted from the most basic business studies textbook. I wondered how much he had plagiarised.

Fortunately, the girls seemed attentive, in that they were sitting still without fidgeting, as Hairnet had trained them to do when we had a guest speaker. But the glazed looks on the faces of the girls I could see told me their thoughts were miles away.

Suddenly, Mr Goldman-Coutts ground to a halt. His tank of platitudes must have run dry, and I was still no wiser as to what his line of business actually was. Did he even work at all? Had he been faking it when he told the bursar that he worked in import/export? His vagueness was very odd.

Mr Goldmann-Coutts turned to Hairnet, who all the while had been standing patiently at his side. At least that would have made it harder for her to doze off. With a flourish of his hand, he yielded the floor to her. She was quick to take his place at the lectern and spoke loudly, with great animation, perhaps attempting to make sure we'd all woken up.

'Mr Goldman-Coutts, thank you so much for that wonderful speech. I'm sure all the girls now can't wait to get cracking on their business projects to put your wise words into practice.'

Like going to bed early? I couldn't see that happening.

'Now, let's all show our appreciation to our esteemed visitor for taking time out of his hectic schedule this afternoon to help the school.' She began to clap enthusiastically, holding her hands high to demonstrate to the girls that they should be doing likewise.

After a few moments of polite applause, Hairnet put her arm through her visitor's and led him towards the door, probably planning to escort him to her study for a thank-you coffee. Herr Ehrlich held back for a moment to wave to his daughter and, sweetly, to blow her a kiss, eliciting the broadest smile I'd seen from her since her arrival.

Then his employer, perhaps realising Herr Ehrlich was in danger of getting left behind, turned to look for him and beckoned to him to catch up. Herr Ehrlich scurried after him. I guessed Hairnet would offer him coffee too. Although he was not paying the fees, he was after all Frieda's father.

Once our visitors had left the room, the girls got to their feet and filed out silently in their usual orderly fashion, bursting into lively chatter the minute they were beyond the assembly hall. They'd soon dispersed, all but Frieda, who lingered dreamily at the back of the hall, fingering her necklace and gazing at the chair at the front of the hall where her father had been sitting during his boss's speech.

What a shame she hadn't been invited to join her father in Hairnet's study. Then I remembered a memo I had written to Hairnet earlier in the day and slipped into my blazer pocket, meaning to drop it off at her study on my way to lunch. I took it out now, glad that I'd put it in an envelope to keep it neat. It wasn't important, only a routine report that she wanted by the end of the following week, but I realised now it might serve another purpose too.

'Frieda.' While the other teachers trooped back wearily to the staffroom, I detoured to speak to her.

'Yes, Miss Lamb?' Her face clouded, as if she was expecting me to tell her off for loitering.

'As you're the only girl here, could you please do me a favour? I have to go to the staffroom now, but Miss Harnett really needs this letter before the next lesson. Would you mind taking it to her study, knocking on her door and delivering it to her by hand? I'd be awfully grateful.'

She beamed at me.

'Of course, Miss. That is easy. I will do it now.'

'Thank you very much, Frieda, I'm most grateful.'

I just hoped Hairnet would get the hint and invite the girl in for coffee with her father and his employer before they headed back to Torrid Manor.

As for me, there was just time for a coffee and to compare notes on our guest speaker's performance with my colleagues before afternoon lessons began.

9

ORIANA WATCHES OUT

'Well, that was a waste of time,' grumbled Mavis, as I closed the staffroom door behind me. 'I could have done a better job than that, and you all know how parlous my financial affairs are. How on earth did that fellow get to be a tycoon?'

'My father used to say, "If he's so smart, why ain't he rich?"' said Judith. 'In his case, I'd switch that around. If he's so rich, why ain't he smart? If indeed he is as rich as he claims.'

Nicolette was more charitable.

'Perhaps he does not know how to speak to people who are not the businessmen, so he down dumbed it, but went too far.'

'Or businesswomen,' added Judith Gosling. 'Maybe he's just used to a male-dominated environment at work and isn't used to being so vastly outnumbered by women. And as he's childless, perhaps he doesn't have much experience with pitching talks to suit teenagers. He did rather over-simplify his address. Our girls would have got more out of something a bit more in-depth.'

Mavis sat down at the central table. 'Perhaps he wasn't dumbing down on purpose. Perhaps he's just stupid, but lucky. The polar opposite of me.'

She smiled through gritted teeth as I took a seat opposite her.

'Even so, Hairnet seems awfully taken with him,' observed Judith, sitting down beside me. 'I thought her introduction rather effusive, considering she couldn't describe anything of substance that he does.'

'Maybe he doesn't do anything but live off the interest of his father's fortune – or his mother's,' I added before Judith could correct me. 'Perhaps he's just the beneficiary of a very big trust fund.'

'In that case, he ought to have found it easier to relate to our girls,' said Mavis. 'I know they're not all TFB, but a lot of their fathers must move in the same circles as him.'

TFB was the St Bride's code for Trust Fund Brigade – the girls whose financial well-being was assured for life by shrewd investments on their behalf by affluent, thoughtful forebears.

'That might explain why he's sponsoring a pupil,' said the bursar, coming to join us around the table, coffee in hand. 'I expect St Bride's was recommended to him by one of our girls' fathers, most likely one of his business acquaintances. Still, I don't see why Miss Harnett is making such a fuss of him. Dozens of fathers of other pupils would have made a much better job of inspiring our young entrepreneurs. Even some of our governors might have done it better.'

That was saying something, considering most of them were doddery ancients who spent most of their meetings eating the lavish lunch with which Hairnet plied them to make them more amenable to her wishes, then sleeping it off in a post-prandial snooze.

I wondered whether the bursar was feeling a little jealous, having only recently revived his romance with Hairnet, but he shouldn't have worried. He must have loved her very much to have stayed loyal to her for all those years that she'd rejected him, after his brief and foolish affair with Piers Goldsworthy's wife. As far as I knew, there'd been no other romantic relationships for either the bursar or Hairnet during all those years of their estrangement. It made me sad to think how much time they had lost, despite working in the same school all along.

But if he was at all jealous now, he shouldn't have been. Hairnet was probably old enough to be Mr Goldman-Coutts' mother, and Hairnet was no cougar.

Suddenly, the staffroom door flew open. Oriana had pushed it far harder than necessary, indicating her heightened level of nervous energy.

'The man's a charlatan,' she declared, striding over to take the cup of coffee the bursar had just poured for himself, even though he hadn't offered it to her. He just sighed and went to help himself to the sludgy dregs of the lunchtime brew, a little smile playing about his lips. Perhaps he was pleased that for once Oriana hadn't been won over by the richest man on her radar.

Joe, browsing the sports pages in his favourite armchair, lowered the newspaper to narrow his eyes at Oriana.

'Why, because he didn't pitch up in a Savile Row suit? Maybe he just likes to spend his money on more worthwhile things than posh clothes. If you're rich enough, you can wear what you like as you don't need to impress anyone any more. I wonder whether I could tap him for a new sports pavilion?'

'You'll have to join the queue,' I said, coming over to join their conversation. I perched on the arm of Joe's chair. 'Hazel's got her eye on him for a new art studio, and I'm rather hoping he'll offer to fund the roof repairs and refurbishment of our flats.'

Oriana pouted.

'Give it up now, my friends. He's wearing a knock-off watch. That's never a real Patek Philippe. Some of the gold had rubbed off its bracelet, on the edge closest to the cuff of his jacket. I'd never date a man who wears a counterfeit watch. You don't know what else he might be faking.'

Joe sniggered.

'Maybe he sold his real designer one to pay Frieda's school fees,' suggested the ever-generous Nicolette. 'The most expensive watches cost hundreds of thousands of pounds.'

'But isn't that how the rich stay rich?' asked Mavis. 'They're notoriously tight-fisted. I bet it's a fake.'

'Some of the girls' parents are very generous to us,' put in Nicolette. 'They give us big presents at Christmas; it is embarrassing.'

'Not too embarrassing for you to accept them, I notice,' replied Mavis curtly, but then she piped down. Perhaps her conscience had got the better of her. She'd been on the receiving end of some expensive gifts from parents herself.

Joe fiddled with the chunky, plastic fitness tracker on his left wrist.

'Maybe that's what his import/export business is built on. Replica designer jewellery from foreign parts. Anyway, he might have a real designer watch at home and just wears a fake one when he goes out on his motorbike. What if the real one flew off while he was bombing along the lanes? He'd never find it again in among the hedgerows.'

'His motorbike?' Oriana froze for a moment, her coffee cup halfway to her lips. 'I thought he had a chauffeur-driven Rolls.'

Joe smirked. 'Don't worry, Oriana, his top-of-the-range Harley-Davidson looks real enough.' He nodded towards the big window that overlooked the forecourt.

'Ugh, motorbikes, I hate them. They're even worse than push-bikes. Helmets play havoc with your hair.'

She returned her coffee, untasted, to the trolley and stalked out of the room. The bursar hastily swapped it for his cup of dregs, and

Nicolette got up to follow him, taking the opportunity to draw to his attention the broken whiteboard in her classroom.

Now we were more or less alone, Joe looked up at me and winked.

'I reckon Oriana's just miffed because she miscalculated her outfit, channelling James Bond's Miss Moneypenny instead of Sandy from *Grease*. She's probably also annoyed that the only person he paid attention to in the audience was Frieda.'

'I noticed that too. It's a strange dynamic, don't you think, the relationship between the three of them – Frieda, her father and his boss? Did you hear what Judith said earlier about Mr Goldman-Coutts being unable to pitch his talk appropriately for the girls because he's childless and not used to dealing with kids, or even with women as a whole?'

'Then if he wants to do something charitable, it seems odd that he'd choose to be a benefactor to a teenage girl,' said Joe. 'Do you suppose there's more to his relationship with the Ehrlichs than meets the eye?'

I considered for a moment.

'Maybe they're former business partners, who have parted company, only for Herr Ehrlich's business to go bust while Mr Goldman-Coutts's flourished. He might feel sorry for Ehrlich, or feel indebted to him for his own success for some reason.'

'Of course, there could be other reasons for the association that have nothing to do with business,' said Joe. 'Perhaps they are long-standing friends or blood relations. Or here's a thought: might he and Herr Ehrlich be in a romantic relationship?'

'That's always a possibility, no matter how unlikely a match they might look. Aren't partners generally equally attractive?'

Joe raised his eyebrows.

'Are you fishing for compliments, Miss Lamb? Are you wanting me say we're both equally gorgeous? Well, you are, anyway.'

I laughed.

'You too, Joe. I think we can agree on that score at least. But back to Herr Ehrlich. I was wondering whether he might have something on his employer?'

'You mean blackmail? If that were the case, I'd expect them to seem less comfortable in each other's presence. If Ehrlich were the blackmailer, I'd expect him to be the more relaxed of the two.'

'Maybe it's just in Herr Ehrlich's nature to be a bit more formal than his boss. That might explain why Frieda seems a bit tense compared to the rest of the girls. He might have raised her in his own image.'

Joe's watch beeped an alarm, and he turned his wrist to show me it was nearly time for the next lesson. The bell would be about to ring to summon us all to our classes.

'That's all food for thought, Joe,' I said, getting to my feet. 'In the meantime, I've got the sixth form next lesson, and I'm looking forward to hearing what they made of Mr Goldman-Coutts.'

10

GIRL TALK

'So what was your take-away from our visitor this afternoon, girls?'
I asked the seventeen-year-olds who had gathered in my classroom
for the first lesson of afternoon school.

'Never wear desert boots with biker gear,' said Sonya, not
missing a beat. 'Honestly, Miss Lamb, I couldn't take my eyes off
them. They were so flipping naff.'

When I pursed my lips in silent admonition, she folded her
arms.

'It's a perfectly valid observation, Miss Lamb, and totally rele-
vant to my business. You see, I'm offering personal fashion advice in
return for a fee. My clients send me photos of themselves in their
favourite outfits, and I write back to tell them their top three styling
mistakes and how to fix them. For example, if they've tucked their
shirt in all the way round, I'll tell them how to do a French tuck
instead.'

When the other girls nodded approvingly, I seized the opportunity to segue into my planned topic for today's lesson.

'You'll need to call on all your persuasive writing skills to phrase your advice diplomatically, so as not to hurt your clients' feelings. How might she do that, girls?'

Tilly raised her hand.

'She could start by saying what she likes about their outfit, or about their looks in general, and say they look lovely, but here's how to look even better.'

'Well done, Tilly, very tactful.'

Sonya immediately picked up on her advice.

'So I could have told Mr Goldman-Coutts that I liked his jacket and boots but not together, for example. Then I could say the white t-shirt was okay but really needed a good wash, and I'd tell him how to adjust his bootlaces to they didn't look like they'd been tied by a five-year-old.'

Before I could respond to that harsh remark, other girls warmed to the topic, calling out further suggestions from around the classroom.

'I'd tell him he's got good hair for his age, but he should part it in the middle, not the side. Or else brush it straight back.'

'I'd say he didn't have many wrinkles considering how old he was, so not to try Botox for another year or two.'

'Do we think he should go darker or lighter with his tan?'

I held up my hands to restore order.

'Girls, please! Can we try to be more positive in our choice of words? Your observations show you gave him your full attention, but I was really hoping to hear your thoughts on what he said to you, rather than on his personal appearance. So, what about the substance of his talk and his style of speaking? Did you spot any persuasive tactics to bring you round to his way of thinking?'

'What substance?' said Eleanor. 'It was all waffle if you ask me. My dad could have done a better talk than that, and he's really boring when he goes on about work.'

'I think you are not kind.'

A reedy, accented voice from the back of the classroom made all the girls turn to stare. In her embarrassment, poor Frieda had made such an effort to make herself inconspicuous, sinking down in her seat in the shady corner at the rear of the room as low as possible without being entirely under the desk. I hoped she wouldn't report this conversation back to him. Although I'd expected the girls to be frank, I hadn't anticipated them to be so brutal.

'Mr Goldman-Coutts is a good, kind man who is helping me and my father. You girls know nothing about his business. That is why you did not think his talk was good.'

I was pleased to hear her speak out so assertively. Perhaps underneath, she wasn't as detached as she appeared. Perhaps she just preferred solitude. Greta Garbo's famous line, delivered in a German accent similar to Frieda's, sprang into my mind: 'I want to be alone'.

Sonya bridled. 'And you do? How come you know so much more about business than we do? You're not even from this country.'

I certainly wasn't going to countenance that comment.

'Sonya! That is an inappropriate remark. Businesses thrive all over the world. Where someone comes from is irrelevant.'

'Yes, Amy in Year 10 is from China and her dad is a brilliant businessman,' chimed in another girl. 'It's a shame her dad couldn't come and give us a talk. He could teach us a thing or two.'

'What is Mr Amy's business?' asked Frieda.

'Dunno. He just buys and sells things.'

'For which the technical term is import and export,' I added. 'I hear that's also Mr Goldman-Coutts' line of business, Frieda?'

The girl rose up in her seat, no longer slouching.

'Yes. I think yes. You could say that.'

'What sort of thing does he import/export?' asked one of the girls. 'Amy's dad is going to send her lots of his stuff to sell for her business. Maybe you could get Mr Goldman-Coutts to do that for yours.'

Frieda shook her head. 'I will make art. I do not need anyone to give me things to sell. I will sell my paintings. Perhaps he will buy some of my paintings. We will make our own art gallery at St Bride's and invite people to buy from it. Perhaps your fathers buy them too.'

If her artistic talent matched her confidence, perhaps that art scholarship was not misplaced after all.

'That's a good idea,' said Sheila. Her support made Frieda sit up even straighter. 'Maybe all of us who are doing Art A Level could stage a selling exhibition? I mean, I've seen worse stuff in Mayfair galleries, near where I live.'

Could Mr Goldman-Coutts be an art dealer, importing and exporting paintings? Well, why not?

'Ooh, yes!' The art students' chorus of approval at Frieda's suggestion snapped me out of my musing. 'Yes, an art business would be easy to set up. We've all got loads of pieces of art in our GCSE portfolios that we've finished with. Let's ask Miss Taylor if we can mount an exhibition. That'll be much easier than inventing or manufacturing something. It'll just be a case of throwing a party and sticking price tags on our pictures. Oh, and thinking of a name for our business so we can advertise it.'

'There's more to it than that,' said Sheila. 'You have to get red sticky dots to put on the pictures when they've been sold. That's what they do in real art galleries. And think of a name for our exhibition.'

'There'll be a catalogue to write, and invitations to draft,' I added. 'Perhaps even a website. Mrs Gosling will help you with that. Lots of opportunities to practice persuasive writing, in any case. Now, who can think of an example of a piece of writing that has persuaded them to buy a product in the past?'

And with that, I managed to steer them onto some serious work, during which Frieda leaned back in her seat looking happy for the first time since she had arrived. I was pleased to observe that at the end of the lesson, instead of hanging back and being left behind by her classmates, as she usually did, they waited for her. As they crossed the courtyard, I saw some of them offering her sweets from their pockets, patting her back or putting their arms through hers.

11

MORE FOR OLIVER

We all seemed to be inventing our own back-stories for Mr Goldman-Coutts. Giving my imagination free rein, I made myself laugh by comparing him to Jay Gatsby, the bootlegger, on dress-down Friday. I'd have to be careful that the next time I saw him, I didn't address him as Mr Gatsby-Coutts.

Only in these post-prohibition days, a Gatsby figure would be more likely to be a drug dealer than a bootlegger. Or perhaps someone who tampered with prescription drugs to make more money, like Harry Lime in *The Third Man*. Being a drug dealer would also count as import and export, even though illegal. What a neat and evasive euphemism. If Mr Goldman-Coutts was a drug dealer, who was to say Frieda wasn't in on the act, and might start dealing among the girls?

Or he might be a money launderer, disposing of money for drug barons. If that was the case, I couldn't see how sponsoring a pupil at St Bride's would help him disguise ill-gotten financial gains, although it might serve as a tax dodge. Surely money launderers only passed on their money to members of their drugs cartel, and I couldn't believe Hairnet or the bursar could be involved in any kind of drug running. On the other hand, all those secret tunnels under the school would make a great place to hide a secret stash of illegally imported drugs before it was distributed to a network of dealers. The school wasn't so desperate for cash that it would become in involved in criminal activities – or was it?

But I dismissed these fanciful notions almost as soon as I'd dreamed them up. I had no evidence – just an overactive imagination. I couldn't accuse any of them of anything untoward. Innocent until proven guilty. The only thing Mr Goldman-Coutts was guilty of was being boring and perhaps not awfully bright.

After so many near-disasters for the school since I joined it the previous September, it was only natural that I should be on my guard. The longer I was here, the more I loved my job – and of course Joe.

It was time to focus on facts – hard, tangible facts – instead of idle speculation.

I gave priority to investigating Sebastian Goldman-Coutts. As the man with the money, he seemed more likely than Herr Ehrlich to be high profile, and his unusual surname worked in my favour, whereas online searches threw up tons of Ehrlichs. He'd likely be the only Sebastian Goldman-Coutts in the world, so he should have been easy to trace online. I was glad I'd had the chance to have a good look at him during his talk, so that I would easily recognise him in any photos a digital search threw up.

To my surprise, my internet searches yielded no trace of Goldman-Coutts, or anyone else of that surname, either locally within the neighbourhood nor in the City of London, where we'd presumed his business interests were based. It seemed I'd have to resort to old technology rather than modern social media. But who in my social circle might have come across him?

The school governors had certainly moved in the right circles, and many of them at the helm of national or global industries, but these days they were all retired. I consulted the school prospectus for the details. Like many successful executives in later life, most had non-executive directorships, but these were all to do with good causes such as public service organisations or registered charities (of which, of course, St Bride's was one).

Personally, I knew only two people who were active in the kind of circles that Mr Goldman-Coutts might move in. Stephen, my ex, had been a rising star in the banking industry while we were together, but even had he not lost his job through a regrettable fall from grace in my first term at St Bride's, I'd have been loath to seek help from him.

The other was a much more recent acquaintance, who also had a vested interest in protecting the school's reputation: Oliver Galsworthy, Oriana's half-brother and the bursar's son.

Strangely, I'd got to know him before they did, when, not long after Christmas, he'd come to the school researching the biography of Piers Galsworthy, the former chair of governors who had died when Oliver was a baby.

Piers was named as Oliver's father on his birth certificate, but his biological father was the bursar – a secret both the bursar and Hairnet had kept from him until then.

When his emails requesting access to the school's archives were rebuffed, Oliver had visited St Bride's in person one Sunday, when I was the only person in school and feeling rather lonely. My planned date with Joe had been cancelled by Oriana whisking him away at the last minute. When the charming and handsome Oliver turned up in a sports car and invited me out to afternoon tea for an informal chat about St Bride's, sad at feeling rejected by Joe, I accepted.

So began a friendship that if it hadn't been for Joe, might have turned into something more. Oliver was easy, pleasant company, and an interesting conversationalist, telling me about his work as a writer, chiefly as a biographer of entrepreneurs, and a business journalist. I'd found him honest and trustworthy in his dealings with the school the previous term, so in his line of work, and with his business connections, he now seemed the perfect person to help me take the next step.

Having spent some time composing a diplomatic and objective email explaining why we would like to know more about Mr Goldman-Coutts, I was startled by the speed of Oliver's reply. He responded almost immediately. I guess someone in his position must constantly have their phone to hand for emails and social media networking, plus a much stronger mobile signal than we have down here in our thick-walled, old building, remote from mobile network masts.

It's astonishing how many rich philanthropists are relatively unknown to the public. Contrary to popular belief, there are relatively few who would like to plaster their private lives across the pages of *Hello!* magazine. Most highly successful, astute businessmen quietly press on with their commercial interests without courting celebrity or public acknowledgement. I'm guessing your Goldman-Coutts is one of those, as I've never come across him before, either. But give me a day or two to put out some feelers, and I'll get back to you with any intelligence I can find as soon as I can. In the meantime, please give my love to Oriana, to my father, and to Caroline too.

So he was calling Hairnet by her first name now, rather than making her an honorary replacement for his late birth mother.

Best love to you too.

He signed the email with his initials and a kiss.

Oh dear. I hoped he wasn't assuming my enquiry was an excuse to contact him again in attempt to pursue the romantic relationship he'd hinted he'd like with me. Hastily, I clicked on my 'sent' box, to reassure myself I hadn't inadvertently added any kisses beneath my signature. The informal protocol of emails, and the speed with which we sent them, made it too easy to foster misunderstanding about relationships.

Although Joe had been perfectly nice about it, and didn't seem to be the jealous type, I still felt guilty for having allowed Oliver for taking me out to tea that day – and embarrassed that, echoing Oriana, I'd been partly attracted, at least initially, by Oliver's smart sports car. All the same, I decided, not to tell Joe that I was back in touch with Oliver, for now, at least.

Nor would I pass on Oliver's fond greetings for the moment, as it would have meant revealing to Oriana, the bursar and Hairnet that I was investigating Goldman-Coutts by proxy. Although my colleagues had teased me for being the school sleuth after the part I'd played in clearing up previous mysteries since I'd joined St Bride's, Hairnet and the bursar might not welcome my enquiries in case they jeopardised the school's relationship with such a valuable sponsor. Oriana might not care, as she had already expressed her own doubts about Mr Goldman-Coutts, but there was no real point in involving her. She'd have nothing to add to any conversation but scorn.

I dashed off a speedy message of thanks to Oliver, adding a Ps.:

Please treat this conversation as strictly confidential – for our eyes only.

He responded with four winking emojis.

I turned off my laptop, then gazed thoughtfully around my poky, temporary flat, with its plain, iron bedstead, humble pine wardrobe and chipped, marble-topped washstand. Yes, a Victorian washstand – that's how basic my new home was. I'd hoped that, being on the top floor, I might have a better view of the magnificent gardens to compensate for the lowering of my living standards. The only window was a tiny skylight set high above my head. All I could see through it was the starless night sky.

Then, to salve my conscience for keeping my correspondence with Oliver a secret from Joe, I went out into the corridor to knock on the door of Joe's flat and invite him to take a nightcap of cocoa with me in the library.

With all the girls tucked up in their dorms, Joe and I had this luxurious, former country gentleman's library to ourselves. We spent a cosy hour cuddled up together on the fireside sofa, the embers of the daytime fire still glowing in the grate.

Afterwards, as we stood outside my door, empty cocoa mugs in my hand, Joe put his arms around me for a sneaky goodnight kiss. I cringed as our empty cocoa mugs clinked together in my hand.

'Let's hope Oriana didn't hear that,' I whispered.

He pulled me closer.

'So what if she does? We're not doing anything wrong. Worst that can happen is that she comes out to tell us to shut up and get a room.'

I forced a smile. How much easier it would have been to be building a new relationship outside of school with someone other than a colleague. Someone like Oliver, perhaps?

'Except we can't get a room, not till the end of term,' I replied. 'You know, it's odd, but last term, it seemed less of a strain for us to go to our separate rooms at the end of the day, even after we'd seen the New Year in sharing a hotel bed. Now every night, I feel as if I'm returning to my prison cell after association time. It'll be like a punishment to climb into that narrow, hard bed alone. I mean, I'm trying hard to make it feel cosy, with pot plants and cushions, and photos around the mirror. Photos of us, that is.'

Joe smiled and kissed the top of my head.

'I'll take that as a tribute to the effectiveness of my former disguise.' He pulled away just enough to look me in the eye, and I saw he was grinning. 'And perhaps to my all-round manliness when I'm just being myself.'

With my mug-free hand, I pulled my flat key out of my pocket and unlocked my front door. The brass fob was the original Victorian one, a relic from the time when the school building was a stately home and was embossed with the words 'scullery maid'.

I closed the door behind me, feeling as if I'd been demoted.

12

ROMANCING GEMMA

As it turned out, it wasn't Oliver that piqued Joe's jealousy but an altogether unexpected fellow. The following Monday, waiting for me in my pigeonhole was a thick, cream, textured envelope with my name written on it in fountain pen. I opened it and pulled out a rigid correspondence card bearing the following message:

You are warmly invited to escort Frieda Ehrlich to join Sebastian Goldman-Coutts for a private supper at Torrid Manor.

So much for my vision of Mr Goldman-Coutts as the ultra-hospitable Gatsby type. A private supper was at the other end of the sociability scale to that tycoon's wild parties. I hoped he wasn't planning a cosy *dîner à deux*.

'A private supper with Mr Moneybags?' said Joe's voice behind me. I hadn't realised he was reading over my shoulder. 'How private a supper? Have any other members of staff been invited?'

Joe began to rifle through the contents of the pigeonholes, but stopped after the third one.

'No, of course not. I'd have spotted the matching envelopes

when I distributed the post this morning. Are you sure the invitation is meant for you, Gemma? Sorry, I don't mean to be rude, but if he was going to invite anyone other than Hairnet or the bursar, I'd have expected him to choose Hazel Taylor, being head of art and Frieda's housemistress.' He gave a lopsided grin. 'Or Oriana, if she applied her feminine wiles.'

I turned the envelope over to check. 'No, it's definitely for me.'

From what Judith had said about Torrid Manor, I'd have gladly transferred my invitation to Hazel or Oriana, but it wouldn't have been good etiquette to field a substitute.

'Shame it's not for Oriana. A posh dinner at a billionaire's house is more her cup of tea than mine. But I'm guessing she'd turn any such invitation down, as she doesn't like him.'

Too late I realised Oriana had sidled up beside Joe and had caught the last part of our conversation.

'Who don't I like?' she said as she read the card. 'Ah, Sebastian. No, quite right. I preferred his chauffeur. He had a certain something about him that his employer completely lacks.'

The corner of Joe's lips twitched mischievously.

'Anything in particular, Miss Bliss?'

She shrugged.

'Oh, just a certain *je ne sais quoi*.'

Joe pointed to a 'Ps.' at the bottom of the card. 'I see he's sending the chauffeur to pick you up, Gemma, so you don't have to worry about drinking and driving. Oriana, if you persuade Gemma to be late getting ready, you might sweet-talk the chauffeur into taking you for a romantic spin round the block in his fancy car while he's waiting.'

Oriana didn't rise to his bait, but just reached for the messages in her own pigeonhole. I wondered whether she was going to check she hadn't received a similar invitation herself, but she just slipped her post into her book bag without letting on.

'Gemma, you'd better get Hairnet's permission to spend the evening out of school,' she said tersely, without looking at me.

I checked the wall calendar.

'Let's see... I'm not on duty that evening anyway, so I think it should be okay – especially as the request has come from Frieda's sponsor. It's not just me trying to bunk off.'

Oriana merely harumphed in reply on her way to the door.

'I hope sending his chauffeur doesn't mean Mr Moneybags is planning to get you sloshed, Gemma,' said Joe after Oriana had left the staffroom. 'He could just as easily have asked you to drive Frieda to Torrid Manor in your car.'

I tucked the invitation inside my planner. 'I make my own decisions on what I drink, thank you very much,' I retorted, trying to make light of it, but Joe seemed unamused.

'So you're going to accept?'

'Yes, of course. I think Hairnet would be cross if I turned him down, don't you? And now that I think about it, it'll be the perfect opportunity to find out more about him. Plus I am curious to see inside his manor house, despite what I said just now about it being wasted on me.' This was true, but I didn't like to betray Judith's confidence by saying why. 'Perhaps I'll come away with a better idea of why he's funding Frieda's education and whether he has any ulterior motive we need to be wary of. Besides, I expect the menu will be rather fancier than St Bride's school dinners, but it's a sacrifice I'm prepared to make.'

Joe glanced at his watch. 'Duty calls. I need to go out to the pavilion and unpack the new lacrosse balls before this afternoon's match. See you later.'

A note of wistfulness had crept into his voice, and as he turned to go, he seemed to have lost a little of his bounce. I thought our conversations about Mr Goldman-Coutts must have made it clear that I was not remotely attracted to him, so I wouldn't have expected him to be jealous of my accepting a dinner invitation from him. Besides, it wasn't as if it was for me alone – I was clearly being asked to tag along only as chaperone, rather than for the pleasure of my company. I was glad now that I hadn't told him about my latest correspondence with Oliver, so as not to make him feel even worse.

I didn't really need to head to my classroom just yet, but I wanted some time alone to think about where my relationship was going with Joe, so I left the staffroom and headed for the courtyard. It wasn't easy, trying to nurture a romantic relationship with a staffroom colleague within the constraints of the school community. Apart from when I was asleep in bed, it was rare to be ever truly on my own at St Bride's. Perhaps that was the real reason for the rule banning staff from having colleagues in their flats. After all her years in the boarding school environment, Hairnet knew that a little time alone was essential for one's sanity – an oasis of solitude amid a storm of enforced company.

Yet as I entered my classroom, it was neither Joe nor Mr Goldman-Coutts that was front of mind, but Oliver Goldsworthy. How much easier it would have been to pursue a romance with Oliver, detached from the daily life of school and unhindered by the weird stop-start nature the school imposed on my relationship with Joe. It was either all systems go in the school holidays or a pretence of the platonic in term-time. Seesawing from one extreme to the other was quite discombobulating.

As for Mr Goldman-Coutts, now that I'd had time to think about his dinner invitation, it made perfect sense for him to have asked me, out of all the staff, to escort Frieda, because I was the only member of staff who spoke any German. I was also the newest member of staff, so might be the most objective about the school, and best able to give him unbiased insights into St Bride's. I resolved to do my best to justify his investment in Frieda's school fees.

I was right about Hairnet's attitude to the invitation. When at the first opportunity I asked her permission to go, she was positively encouraging.

'Well done, my dear. The more we can do to befriend Mr Goldman-Coutts, the better,' she replied. 'Besides, it will be a treat for Frieda to have a little outing of her own to see her sponsor, and the car ride will give her more time to spend with her father without her sponsor there to play gooseberry. Just let Max know so that he's ready to unlock the school gates on your return.'

When I passed this on to Max, he withdrew a large mobile phone with a military-strength protective rubber casing from one of the many pockets of his combat trousers.

'And if we don't return by midnight, could you come to our rescue?' I asked him when he passed me in the courtyard on my way to my next lesson.

'Okay, Cinderella,' he replied. That he was so relaxed about the invitation took the edge off my nerves. 'Text Joe your ETA so he can unlock the front door for you. I'll take care of the gates. I'll make sure I'm at my lodge at the right time to let you in.'

13

ROMANCING JOE

Wanting to reassure Joe that I didn't view my visit to Torrid Manor as a date, I suggested we take a stroll in the school grounds after the last lesson of the afternoon to see how the spring bulbs were progressing. I was ashamed of how seldom I took time to appreciate the beautiful setting of the school estate. Had I been staying at a place like this on holiday, I'd have explored the gardens every day and got to know them far better in a week than I knew St Bride's gardens after six months in residence.

The chilly, wintry weather and short, dark days had deterred me from many walks in the grounds since the turn of the year, but now we were in late February and the daylight hours outlasted the school timetable, the prospect of a stroll at the end of each day was becoming much more appealing.

There was just enough time before the supper bell rang for a half-hour's walk. As Joe and I left the building and followed the neat, gravelled path through the immaculate formal gardens past creamy, classical statuary, I took a deep breath and held it. It was my first proper taste of fresh, outdoor air all day, apart from crossing between the main school building and the classroom courtyard. That didn't really count as you couldn't see the stunning gardens from the courtyard. After all, the courtyard had once been the stable block, plain and functional for the housing of horses and the storage of carriages. Only once inside the classrooms could you see greenery through the far windows, which gave tantalising views across to the towering trees – planted in Lord Bunting's day and now striking, mature specimens. Many of them were now dappled with pink or white blossom. As we approached the lake, buttery primroses and scarlet cyclamen began to pepper the velvety lawns, and as we entered light woodland, I spotted luscious lime-green buds heralding the imminent emergence of daffodils, then wild garlic and bluebells. How fragrant the spring here would be!

Yet when seated at my desk, I had my back to all this, so the luscious landscape never distracted me. While immersed in teaching or marking, it was too easy to forget what lay beyond my classroom.

Spending time in the gardens with Joe was even more appealing than walking alone. As we strolled along together now, I thrust my hands in my skirt pockets to make sure I didn't slip my hand into Joe's without thinking, where pupils might see us.

As we headed for the lake, I turned to Joe.

'Although all the bulbs have yet to flower, it really smells as if spring is on its way now, doesn't it?'

He lifted his chin to sniff the air, like a hunting dog getting its bearings on its master's prey.

'Yes, it does. Although I'm used to it with most of my lessons outdoors, I hadn't articulated that yet. Not that I have spring flowers on my sports pitches to prompt such thoughts.'

He pointed to a splash of cerise cyclamen, its bird-like flowers bright above the matte, mottled grey-green leaves.

'Just as well, really. No spring flowers would last long on the playing fields at the front of the school, with dozens of lacrosse boots marauding across them every day.'

'I thought St Bride's winter sport was hockey, not lacrosse? Don't schools usually play one or the other?'

Joe shook his head. 'No, hockey was last term. This term we're onto lacrosse. It's Hairnet's frog-kissing sports strategy.'

I stopped in my tracks to stare at him.

'She has the girls kissing frogs on the playing fields? Surely all the frogs are on this side of the grounds, by the lake?'

Joe laughed.

'No, silly, I'm talking metaphorically.' He hesitated. 'I do mean metaphor, don't I, Miss Lamb? That is the right technical term?'

'That depends entirely on your explanation. Tell me more.'

Although his teasing tone made me smile, I was secretly touched by Joe's continuing efforts to take an interest in my subject.

As we left the gravel path to stroll down the gentle incline through light woodland down to the lake, he laid a hand gently on the small of my back as we crossed rougher ground, ready to catch me if I stumbled. Once we'd reached the level, grassy path that wound around the lake, he took his hand away again and slipped both hands into the pockets of his scarlet hoodie. It reminded me of the cheery colour of tulips, although it was too early for tulips in the gardens just yet.

'But you're right, it's unusual for a school to offer both hockey and lacrosse as they're similar in lots of ways. It means doubling up on kit and having less time to master the skills of each sport, too. But Hairnet insists that we give the girls the opportunity to sample as many sports as possible, in the hope of finding at least one that they'll love and enjoy for the rest of their lives. Like frogs and princes in the fairy tale, you know?'

Hairnet's innovations constantly impressed me.

'I wish I'd had opportunities like that at my high school. I've yet to find my prince. In terms of sports, anyway,' I added, feeling mean now for teasing him.

Thankfully, there had been no rain that day, and it was too early for dew to form, so the bench was dry enough to sit on. We settled back comfortably to enjoy the view, which contained an unexpected new feature.

I pointed to a small, wooden rowing boat tied to a stake just beyond the bench. 'Oh look, where did that come from?'

Joe leapt to his feet and strode over to inspect it.

'It's one of the St Bride's harbingers of spring,' he announced. 'The gardeners must have just brought it out of the boathouse.' He stepped aboard and turned to face me. 'Come on, Gemma, let's have a little row, shall we? I love rowing.'

I hesitated, looking down at my knee-length, straight, brown skirt and buff suede court shoes. Practical, plain clothes for the classroom, as ever, but not ideal for boating.

'Come on, Miss Lamb. It's allowed, honest, for staff, anyway. Only the girls have to ask permission to take the boat out. And it's perfectly dry and clean, if that's what's holding you back.'

I gave in, the appeal of a romantic boat trip with Joe outweighing my fear of spoiling my shoes.

He held out his hand to help me keep my balance as I stepped down from the shore into the boat. We both settled down on the narrow bench seats, and, seizing the oars, he pushed us off from the side and began to row.

A few ducks were scudding in the spring sunshine against a backdrop of sloping banks dotted with clusters of delicate snowdrops, mauve crocuses, and butter-yellow winter aconite.

'This view would make a great jigsaw puzzle,' I observed. 'Now there's a gift of a business idea for any girls who have yet to dream up one of their own.'

Deftly manoeuvring around the little island that held the duck house, Joe nodded.

'We might suggest that any of the girls who live in fancy properties do that for their own homes. Maybe Frieda Ehrlich could do one of Torrid Manor. What do you reckon?

I grimaced.

'From what Judith tells me about it, it wouldn't be the best example.'

Joe raised his eyebrows in surprise.

'Why, what does she say about it? I assumed it must be dead posh, if he's a billionaire. You know, the sort of place you see featured in fancy lifestyle magazines, or celebrity gossip rags.'

I leaned forward until our knees were touching, mine sandwiched between his. After glancing about us to make sure no one was watching, Joe lowered the oars and bent to kiss me on the lips, and I laid my hands on his knees. I determined to enjoy the physical contact with Joe while I could.

'Judith reckons Torrid Manor is uninhabitable. That it would need hundreds of thousands of pounds, if not millions, to make it fit for human occupation. The work would take months or possibly years to complete, especially as it's a listed building. English Heritage would have to approve the process every step of the way, as they do with repairs to the school.'

Joe raised his eyebrows in surprise.

'How does Judith know? Has she been there? Has Goldman-Coutts already had her over? Blimey, he's a fast worker.'

I laughed.

'Yes, but she wasn't there as his guest. She went there before he moved in. Apparently, she's been dating an estate agent in Tetbury.'

Joe rested the right oar and paddled only with the left one to turn the boat around.

'She's kept that quiet. But now I think of it, I did wonder why I'd seen her going into Dixon and Sons when I was cycling through Tetbury last term. I assumed she must be looking to buy or rent a place of her own around here to use in the school holidays. She's got a flat in Wales somewhere that's been her permanent base outside term-time, and I thought it seemed odd that she might think of trading it in for a place around here, where property is so much more expensive. But it seems she's after quite a different asset.'

I grinned. 'Well, good for her. Dating an estate agent comes with certain perks, apparently. She was telling me he takes her on private property viewings just for fun, to feed her interest in local history and architecture. Apparently, her thesis at university was on the impact of the medieval wool trade on the Cotswolds. As I expect you know, rich wool merchants built masses of interesting old residences round here and also funded the expansion and embellishment of many parish churches. So this Roger takes her out to see any historic properties that come onto his books. They take a picnic and pretend these places are theirs for the day. It sounds great fun, don't you think?'

'Very romantic. Provided it doesn't get him into trouble with his boss if he gets found out. Although fear of discovery might add a certain frisson of excitement to their outings.'

He began to row with both oars again, pulling evenly and gently so that we passed steadily through the water. I thought about his arm muscles, firm beneath the long sleeves of his sports hoodie. I doubted Oliver would be able to row as powerfully as this, or indeed to perform any sport as well as Joe.

'I don't think we need worry about his job. His surname is Dixon – presumably he's the "and Son".'

Joe's lips twitched in amusement. 'So are you hinting that I should take you out for a secret slap-up meal in my sports pavilion one day?'

I laughed. 'Surrounded by all that smelly old sports equipment? Thanks, but no thanks.'

Joe's pavilion had a powerful and distinctive aroma: a blend of dubbin, leather, wood and rope, with a touch of dried mud and wet grass. In the hands of an expert perfumier, that combination might be manipulated into a rugged aftershave, but left to itself, it was an appetite suppressant.

'Anyway, let me tell you more about Torrid Manor. I've been picking Judith's brains about it, and it's all very odd.'

'Okay, fire away.'

'Apparently it fell derelict during the last years of its previous owner's life. When he died, he left it to his only living relative, a permanent resident of Barbados. This heir wasn't interested, never visited it, and let it fall into disrepair.'

'He must have been very rich to disregard a historic manor in his property portfolio.'

'Or too poor to fly over here and fix it up, or to commission anyone else to do so for him. Anyway, some years later, he died, and left it to someone else who lived in Hong Kong. That person just wanted rid of it before it became a complete liability. By now the place had got very overgrown, a few ceilings had collapsed, and it was riddled with rot and mould.'

'Perhaps not quite as romantic a setting for Judith and her chap as we'd pictured it. So was it him who sold it to Mr Moneybags? Doesn't sound like much of a business investment to me.'

I realised he was steering us back to the mooring post, and I was sorry our boat trip was so short. Joe may not have had a fancy sports car like Oliver's, but it was hard to beat an open boat on a scenic lake for romance, or the cycle rides we often shared on our days off through the Cotswold country lanes.

Now the sun was low in the sky, it was starting to feel chilly, exacerbated by the cold, damp air above lake. I pulled my scarf a little more tightly around my neck.

'Here's the funny thing. Judith says Roger called Torrid Manor a complete lemon. When he'd first taken it on, he even had to send some foresters in to hack a parting in the undergrowth to make the house accessible from the drive. Plus there was no central heating, or indeed heating of any kind, only vast, old, open fireplaces. I don't suppose the plumbing was up to much, either.'

Joe grinned as he brought the oars into the boat and stood up to loop the painter line around the mooring post. 'The sort of property estate agents describe as "ripe for restoration". Still, I expect there are grants available for the restoration of listed buildings. Doubtless a businessman like Mr Moneybags could get his accountant to offset a lot of the costs against tax.'

He stepped nimbly onto the grassy bank then turned to reach both hands to help me ashore.

'But it still makes no sense. Judith says the final sale only happened just after the New Year. When she went for her picnic there with Roger, it was just before Christmas, and Roger reckoned it would take months, if not years, to make it habitable.'

Joe let out a low whistle as we returned to sit on the bench.

'That explains why Mr Moneybags wasn't on Oriana's radar if he's only just moved in. Nonetheless, you'd think it wouldn't be ready to live in for months if what Roger said is true. To be honest, I don't envy you your visit after all. You'd better wrap up warm for it, and possibly eat before you go.'

'Don't you think it's all a bit odd? He's apparently hugely rich from no apparent cause and moves in at short notice to a derelict house not fit for human habitation?'

Joe shrugged.

'Rich people can afford to be odd. Maybe he grew up in a

draughty old castle and it reminds him of his childhood home. I'm guessing he's no townie softie like you.'

I laughed and gave his thigh a playful slap.

'But seriously, I am a bit worried about going there on my own. I even wondered whether it's a front, and the chauffeur's under instructions to take me somewhere completely different, to some secret location that is Mr Goldman-Coutts' real home. Or do you think I am being silly? To be fair, I told Max about it and he seemed unconcerned.'

'Well, there's your answer. If Max is happy for you to go, then so am I. Although of course, Max's perspective will be purely dispassionate, as he's not your boyfriend.'

I smiled.

'No worries there, Joe. Mr Goldman-Coutts is no more my type than he is Oriana's. Anyway, I'm starting to look forward to it now, as it'll give me the perfect opportunity to find out more about him and the whole set-up with the Ehrlichs. He may not have given much away about himself or about them when he came to give his talk, but I'm sure I'll be able to find out more about him by seeing him on his own territory, and how they interact together when they're at home.'

'Yes, it will be interesting to see how it pans out. For example, will the dinner be all four of you sitting down together, or is it really an invitation for Frieda to eat in the servants' quarters with her father? Or is it more for the benefactor to assess how Frieda is getting on, to help him decide whether his investment is worthwhile?'

'Good point,' I said, shifting in my seat. My spine was beginning to feel chilled by the cold, wooden bench, despite the warmth of Joe's arm around me. I pulled back my coat sleeve to check my watch. 'I'll definitely keep a close watch on them – body language as well as words – to try to work out just what is going on there.'

Joe's fitness tracker began to beep, and he pressed a button to silence it before getting to his feet and reaching for my hands to haul me up.

'Come on, we'd better back indoors. It'll be supper time soon.'

The warmth of his hands made me realise I was shivering.

'The Trough will feel tropical compared to the inside of Torrid Manor.'

I squeezed his hands affectionately before dropping them for the sake of appearances. As we retraced our steps around the lake, I could see on the lawns in the distance a few of the younger girls having an invigorating game of chase prior to the supper bell. Their cheeks were rosy with exertion.

'I guess that's why the dress code on the invitation said "casual". I'll make sure I wear plenty of layers, and if he's managed to rig up some decent heating in the meantime – or Judith's wrong about the primitive conditions – I can always just peel things off as the evening goes by.'

Joe grinned. 'Like a human game of pass the parcel.'

'Hmm, I'm not so sure about that!' I laughed. 'But I'll look forward to telling you all about it on my return. How about a post-mortem over cocoa when I get back?'

He wiggled his eyebrows in the manner of a silent movie villain. 'As long as you survive your ordeal.'

I grimaced.

'No, seriously, that would be grand,' he added.

Just then, the girls on the lawn spotted us and waved, and one belted across to Joe, her arms outstretched in front of her.

'Tag! You're it, Mr Spryke!'

She dashed away, screeching and giggling.

Joe emitted a roar and broke into a run, scattering the gaggle of girls in all directions across the lawn, like a cat attempting to ambush a flock of sparrows.

14

CHAUFFEUR SERVICE

The following week, taking Mr Goldman-Coutts at his word and bearing Judith's advice in mind, on the evening of my invitation to dinner, I dressed casually in wide, navy-blue, corduroy trousers (over tights, socks and brown, fleece-lined ankle boots for warmth) and a pale-lemon, roll-necked sweater (over thermal vest and long-sleeved, cream t-shirt). For good measure, I added a midnight-blue pashmina dotted with tiny golden stars, a Christmas gift from one of my Year 9 pupils.

To compensate for the casual style, I made sure I was very well groomed. I'd washed my hair and pinned it up in a loose, elegant bun, and polished my boots until they shone. With fresh make-up and a spray of scent, I felt as presentable as could be after a hard day's work.

As I watched out of the staffroom window for my chauffeur to arrive, I felt like Cinderella, and not only because of Max's jokey comment. Oriana, seated on the sofa, lowered the *Times Educational Supplement* to look me up and down, her gaze finally falling on the lemon sweater.

'I just hope he doesn't serve you anything in a tomato sauce or raspberry coulis. It'd be hell to get stains out of such a pale, fine-knit sweater.'

Irritated that she could dash my confidence so easily, I didn't reply, but then I realised that by Oriana's standards, her comment counted as a compliment on my choice of top.

When twin glowing orbs appeared like an alien spaceship at the far end of the drive, and I realised my chauffeur was approaching. Without more ado, I grabbed my tan, leather clutch bag and headed to the entrance hall, where Frieda, snug in a dark-green, woollen coat, was waiting for me on the sofa.

The bursar was hovering nearby, waiting to lock the door for the evening after our exit.

'We can't leave the door open all night and put one hundred girls at risk of an intruder,' he observed. I suspected he wanted to reassure Frieda as much as me. 'Just make sure you lock it again on your return.'

'We will,' I replied with a nervous smile.

I'd expected Herr Ehrlich to come to the door, but after waiting by the front door for a few moments, it was clear I was mistaken, so I took the initiative and stepped outside. He was sitting in the front of his employer's Rolls-Royce, engine gently purring. Through the open front door, I beckoned Frieda to follow, and she sprinted across the marble floor in her enthusiasm to see her father at last, and ran ahead of me to greet him. As I heard the bursar lock the door behind us and shoot the bolts across, I felt like a convict leaving prison at the end of her sentence, cast adrift in the scary, outside world, and missing the security of incarceration.

Although quite a few lamps were on in the rooms at the front of the house, heavy curtains drawn tightly for insulation blocked most of the light.

Since I'd left the staffroom, someone had closed the wooden

shutters, so that the light that had flooded into the forecourt from that source was masked.

I blinked to help my eyes adjust to the darkness. Herr Ehrlich had parked Mr Goldman-Coutts' Rolls-Royce about ten paces from the portico, instead of drawing up beside it. Had he never collected anyone from a porticoed mansion before? Did he not realise the purpose of the portico was to spare the traveller exposure to the elements? That seemed odd in a chauffeur to a billionaire tycoon with a mansion of his own.

It didn't deter Frieda, however, who had already climbed into the front passenger seat and was chatting animatedly to her father. She must have been glad to be able to converse in her native language after weeks of operating only in English.

As I stepped out briskly from beneath the portico, the gravel crunching under my boots, the motion-sensitive light came on. I was thankful that it stayed illuminated until I was inside the car, although this process took me longer than it should have done. Realising Herr Ehrlich wasn't going to step out of the car to open the door for me – after all, I was effectively a fellow employee rather than his employer – I grabbed the rear left passenger door handle and tried to open the door.

No joy. Embarrassed by my ineptitude, I let go of the handle, stretched and wriggled my fingers like a pianist limbering up, and tried again. Nothing. I bent down to peer inside the car. What was going on? Herr Ehrlich appeared to be absorbed in his conversation with his daughter. Although it seemed a shame to interrupt their family reunion, I had no choice but to tap on the window for his attention until he turned round to look at me. As best I could, I mimed my dilemma through the glass, pointing to the door handle and turning my clenched fingers back and forth as if applying a key. When at last, it dawned on him that I couldn't get in, he raised a forefinger and mouthed what looked like an 'Aha!' to me, before leaning forward to search the dashboard for the central locking button.

The night air was colder than I'd anticipated – it was only early March, after all – and I began to shiver. I was just wondering whether Herr Ehrlich had forgotten about me when he reached to the far side of the complicated dashboard and pressed a button, triggering the unmistakeable click of the car door lock being released.

Now I was able to haul the door open with relative ease for its substantial weight. I knew Rollers were well built, but this one felt positively armoured. But then I'd never been inside one before. I was used to driving an economical, compact hatchback. It was as similar to a Rolls as a pushbike to a Harley-Davidson.

'*Vielen Dank, Herr Ehrlich*,' I said as I settled myself into the seat and fastened the safety belt. He smiled at me in the rear-view mirror and twirled his hand in the kind of regal wave our late Queen was famous for. His lips moved as he waved, but no sound came out. Or rather, it probably did, but I couldn't hear a word, because, I now realised, a glass panel divided the driver's cab from the rear passenger seats. The sliding communications hatch was shut. *Fair enough*, I thought; Frieda wouldn't want her teacher eaves-dropping on her conversation with her father. This wasn't Parents' Night.

Herr Ehrlich immediately began to accelerate down the drive far faster than I'd ever seen anyone take it before, undaunted by the lack of lighting. I realised the only artificial light on the drive and on the country lanes that led to Torrid Manor would be his head-lights and those of any other cars on the road.

Fortunately, we were unlikely to encounter any cars coming towards us on the single-track drive at this time of night, which was just as well as he was going too fast to brake safely if one did suddenly appear. I gave a sigh of relief when he screeched to a halt between the lodge houses at the gate, where the drive reached the main road. I wondered if their residents, Max Security on the left and the bursar on the right, were watching us.

If they were, they'd have had to be quick not to miss us. Herr Ehrlich didn't stop long enough to check properly for oncoming traffic in either direction before pulling out so fast that the tyres squealed on the tarmac.

Fearing for our lives, I slumped back in my seat and closed my eyes, not caring any more about the risk of offending Herr Ehrlich. While he and Frieda seemed oblivious to the danger – they were too absorbed in animated conversation – I was preoccupied with my own safety, gripping the handle above the door with my left hand and the thick, leather arm rest with my right to brace myself against the swerving motion of the car. I hoped whatever was on tonight's menu at Torrid Manor was highly digestible, otherwise I didn't rate its chances of staying in my stomach on the return journey.

The sustained blaring of a horn passing us on my left made my eyes snap open. This road had only one lane in each direction. Had Herr Ehrlich just made a reckless overtake? I glanced behind me. Nope, the only car in the road was travelling away from us.

Then it dawned on me: Herr Ehrlich was driving on the right - the wrong side for us - forcing the other car to swerve to avoid a collision.

My hand shot to the knob on the communications panel, and I wrenched it open.

'Herr Ehrlich, Herr Ehlich, please drive on the left. *Bitte am links fahren. Links fahren!* Keep left, if you please. We drive on the left in this country!'

It's amazing how the long-lost dregs of schoolgirl languages can rise to the top of your mind *in extremis*.

He broke into a broad smile, revealing huge, sturdy, yellowing teeth.

'*Ach so! Es tut mir leid, gnädige Frau!*' He thumped his forehead with the heel of his palm. '*Gott in Himmel, ich habe es ganz vergessen!*'

His apology did not assuage my fear, even though he phrased it so elegantly, calling me 'Gracious lady', and I found his claim that he'd simply forgotten to drive on the left astounded me.

The rest of his speech was lost on me as he rabbited away in an even more thickly accented German than Frieda's. I sat back once more, exhausted by the adrenalin surge.

Mercifully, we encountered no other cars for the rest of our journey down winding, single track lanes. At least the sole carriageway meant we couldn't drive on the wrong side again.

My heart rate had just about returned to normal when abruptly, we swerved to the right as he made what felt like an emergency stop at a pair of ornamental, wrought-iron gates built into high, drystone walls stretching away into the darkness on either side of us. Herr Ehrlich climbed out of the car, producing a huge, black key from his pocket to unlock the gates, before driving just beyond them and braking sharply again. While he got out to lock the gates behind us, I leaned forward, squinting as I tried to make out the manor house ahead. If we were almost there, it might be safer to leap out of the car now and run the rest of the way. But on this moonless night, all I could see was an unkempt hedge about ten feet tall, stretching into the distance on either side. I suspected it might even surround the estate entirely: a secondary defensive device inside the outer wall.

A few metres ahead of us was the only breach I could see in the hedge – a roughly-hewn square cutting just tall and wide enough to admit a small truck. There was not yet any sign of the manor house, nor of any kind of habitation. I closed my eyes again and surrendered myself to doing the rest of the journey by car. After all, Herr Ehrlich didn't mean me any harm – did he? It wasn't as if he was a kidnapper, abducting me into a secret wilderness for some unspeakable purpose. There were far more valuable kidnapping targets at the school than me.

Just then, my seatbelt cut across my chest so hard that I anticipated a bruise. But the injury was a small price to pay if it meant this terrifying journey had ended.

Herr Ehrlich switched off the engine, leapt from his seat, and ran round the front of car to open the front passenger door. Frieda leapt into his arms for a bear hug, then with his arm around her, the pair strolled away into the darkness.

Then the right rear passenger door flew open, and as I looked up, Oliver Galsworthy beamed down on me.

15

THE UNEXPECTED GUEST

'Hello, Gemma, how lovely to see you again.'

My head spinning, I unclipped my seat belt and leapt out of the car. Giddy after the turbulent journey, I half fell into Oliver's open arms, then stepped back quickly, hoping he didn't interpret it as an affectionate embrace.

'Welcome to Torrid Manor. Good journey?' His lips twitched in amusement at the expression on my face. 'Our bountiful host has just been regaling me with a vivid description of his chauffeur's unusual driving technique. Sounds as if in his former life he must have been a rally driver. Come inside and have a drink. I'm sure you need one.'

No motion sensitive lights came on, but Oliver switched on his mobile phone's torch function to light our way. When I stumbled in a pothole in front of the portico, he took my arm, and I allowed him to lead me towards the imposing front door of the shabby, Elizabethan pile that Judith had described.

Torrid Manor looked even darker than St Bride's, with only a single chink of light showing where the front door was ajar. The door opened into a square, low-ceilinged hall from which an old, oak staircase doglegged up to a galleried landing. Beyond the pool of light from Oliver's phone, everything lay in darkness.

'The only electricity supply here is ancient and sparse, and there's no gas at all as the house is too far from the nearest mains. But don't worry, the room where supper is being served is bright enough, and less cold than you might expect for an old house with no central heating.'

I noticed Oliver was wearing a thick scarf over his tweed jacket and pullover, and he showed no intention of removing them now we were indoors.

We entered a larger room with a much higher ceiling and, as far as I could tell in the near-darkness, what looked like a minstrels' gallery at one end. As we began to cross it diagonally, I put my hand on Oliver's chest to halt him.

'Before we go in there, please tell me what you're doing here, Oliver? I know you kindly agreed to research Mr Goldman-Coutts credentials for me, but I wasn't expecting you to pitch up on his doorstep. I hope you haven't told him I put you up to it.'

He grinned. 'Don't worry, I've been very discreet and ethical. I'm no tabloid trickster. When I drew a blank from all the usual sources – Companies House, and so on – I simply took the approach I often use when one of the papers I work for asks me to interview an important businessman. I wrote him a nice, old-fashioned letter in my best handwriting and in fountain pen, and asked for an hour of his time at the most convenient place for me to interview for a press profile. A handwritten letter will often get you noticed where email doesn't, not least because letter boxes don't have spam filters. You just need to know where your target lives, and you'd given me his address. The rest was like child's play. I gave the impression that I would give him an easy ride – that it was for the sort of piece that ends up as one of those hackneyed, "A Sunday in the Life of (insert role model's name here)" articles. Even the shyest entrepreneur finds that kind of offer hard to refuse. He immediately got his PA to call me and invite me to dinner here tonight.' He put his hand to his mouth. 'Actually, I've just twigged – I think it must have been that chauffeur who called me, as it was a man with an Eastern European accent.'

'It's some kind of regional German dialect, but I haven't yet worked out which one. But yes, pretty hard to understand. The chauffeur's name is Herr Ehrlich, by the way, and Mr Goldman-Coutts is paying his daughter Frieda's school fees. I didn't tell you any more about the Ehrlichs when I asked you to research Mr Goldman-Coutts. Their name is so common that I didn't think you'd be able to find out anything about them. But I thought you might know our host here, or at least know about him or know someone who knows him.'

Oliver raised his eyebrows in puzzlement.

'So is it because of his sponsorship that you want to know more about him? I just assumed he was the father of a prospective pupil.'

'It's complicated. I'll tell you more later.' I waved a hand at him dismissively. 'So have you got anything interesting out of him that you might turn into a news story?'

'Nope. I think this is a bit of a wild goose chase for me in terms of journalistic potential, unless he's saving a juicy secret up his sleeve that he's planning to share with me later.'

Not wanting to give him the wrong idea by lingering alone in the dark – I wanted a clear conscience when later I told Joe about bumping into Oliver unexpectedly – I motioned towards the direction of the door at the far corner of the room, which was showing an alluring chink of light.

'We'd better not keep our host waiting any longer,' I said, starting to walk towards it.

Oliver fell into step beside me.

'By the way,' I said. 'I had no idea that you'd be invited on the same night as me until he told me just now. But I'm jolly glad to see you all the same.'

'Same here. I couldn't believe my luck. When he told me he'd invited a teacher from St Bride's to dinner, I asked which one, and he told me your name. I was so pleased it was you. And when I told him I knew you, it seemed natural to volunteer to venture out into the cold, dark night to escort you in, to save taking him away from his glowing hearth. Which gave me the perfect opportunity to fill you in. It's amazing how much you can manipulate powerful people just by asking nicely. Now, come on. He'll have heard our footsteps stopping and he'll wonder what we're up to. Probably thinks I've waylaid you for a passionate kiss.'

I hoped that wasn't a hint. I wondered what he'd told our host about his relationship with me?

He pointed skywards. 'Let's pretend I've just been showing you the remarkable vaulted ceiling, reputed to include wood recycled from Spanish ships sunk when the English thrashed the Spanish Armada.' He slipped his hand under my elbow to guide me across the rest of the room. 'I suppose at a pinch I might try pitching a house makeover piece to a property editor, once the work's complete.'

'You know, I really must read up on the Spanish Armada,' I said loudly as we approached the dining room door. 'When I get back, I'll ask our history teacher, Judith Gosling, to recommend a good book on the subject from the school library.'

Oliver pushed the door open in front of me, then stood back to allow me to precede him into the room.

For a moment, I stood blinking as my eyes adjusted to the relative brightness of the candlelight that flickered above a long, oak, Jacobean-style table, dark as mahogany from centuries of use. Our host was dressed in an old-fashioned silk smoking jacket over a dinner suit, reminding me of a country squire from a Jeeves novel.

He was smiling at us benignly from the far end of the table, where he sat on an imposing wooden throne, carved all over with scrolls and flowers and fruit.

'Miss Lamb, welcome to Torrid Manor.'

Mr Goldman-Coutts motioned to a slightly smaller throne positioned halfway along the table, facing the open fire blazing in the huge, inglenook fireplace.

Oliver followed me to pull the heavy chair out from beneath the table, beckoned me to sit down and gently, pushed it from behind to move me closer to the elaborate place setting. The chair seemed so heavy, I doubt I could have repositioned it by myself. I took quick stock of the cutlery: enough for soup, entrée, dessert, and cheese. I was glad I'd chosen my loosest fitting trousers.

As Oliver went to resume his seat at the opposite end of the table, facing Mr Goldman-Coutts, footsteps pattered towards us across the room with the Armada ceiling. A moment later, Herr Ehrlich appeared in the doorway, panting. He locked eyes with Mr Goldman-Coutts, who smiled and nodded.

'*Ich bringe es gleich*,' said Ehrlich, or something like that, before tripping back across the hall. He'd bring it straight away. But what had he done with Frieda?

'So, welcome, Miss Lamb,' Mr Goldman-Coutts said again. 'Thank you so much for escorting Frieda. I've given her father permission for a private dinner with her, so I hope you won't mind joining me with your fellow guest, the distinguished journalist and biographer Oliver Galsworthy?' It sounded as if Oliver had rather exaggerated his career achievements in order to secure his interview.

I smiled in thanks. 'I'm honoured. This is such a treat.' I cast my hand about to indicate the splendid setting.

He nodded in acknowledgement.

'Plus, when Frieda told me that you are teaching the girls the art of persuasive writing, I thought what could be better experience for you than to see a professional journalist in action? An experience you may share with the girls. And a delight for us both to have the pleasure of your company, of course.' He turned to Oliver. 'I've had good reports from Frieda on Miss Lamb's teaching.'

Herr Ehrlich scurried back into the room and from Mr Goldman-Coutts' end of the table, seized a bottle of wine in each hand, each of them already half empty.

'*Rot oder weiss, gnädige Frau?*'

'Red or white,' I translated for Oliver, before stating my preference.

'*Weiss, bitte.*'

I wondered how Herr Ehrlich, with his almost non-existent English, would have coped with the complex school registration form for his daughter.

Once he'd filled my glass almost to the brim, he went to top up Oliver's. Oliver put his hand over his half-full glass of white.

'Just water for me from now on, please. I have to drive back to London tonight.'

So he'd come under his own steam, rather than being chauffeured. In the darkness outside, I hadn't spotted his car. I wondered whether Frieda would mind if I asked Oliver to drop us off on his way home, rather than submitting to her father's driving again.

I didn't like the way Herr Ehrlich was eyeing the remains of the bottles of wine, almost salivating. Perhaps he'd even been imbibing prior to collecting me from St Bride's? That might explain his uninhibited driving. Perhaps where he came from, drink-driving was not illegal. Even so, it was inexcusable if it was drink that made him such a bad driver. That might also have been the reason he kept the glass panel closed, so that I couldn't detect the alcohol fumes on his breath. I wondered how long it would take me to walk back to St Bride's.

I was even beginning to wonder about Herr Ehrlich's competence as a single parent. Perhaps he had taken to drink to comfort himself for the loss of his late wife. For Frieda's sake, I was glad Mr Goldman-Coutts had stepped up as her sponsor. I vowed to be kinder to Frieda in future, no matter how abrasive her behaviour.

16

TWENTY QUESTIONS

As I'd anticipated, on his home turf, Mr Goldman-Coutts seemed so much slicker and self-assured than when standing in front of one hundred girls, attempting to inspire them. Oliver's flattering tone as he plied our host with questions over our four-course meal made him relax and open up, although when Oliver finally closed his notebook halfway through our dessert, I realised that Mr Goldman-Coutts had said nothing of substance about his career – named no companies, nor referred to any particular products or deals. He'd just issued general platitudes similar to the advice he'd given the girls. Nothing that he said was exactly suspicious, and it was the kind of thing you could only agree with – citing Mr Micawber's principle of solvency, for example. But nor did it pin him down. Import/export, that nebulous, catch-all phrase, had peppered the conversation, but he'd never specified just what he was trading in.

I didn't know how many answers Oliver had managed to get out of him before my arrival, but I thought it worth quizzing him myself, to make the most of this opportunity to get to know more about him. However, every time I asked him a question, he side-stepped it and returned a meaningless platitude.

'Does your business take you abroad much, Mr Goldman-Coutts?' I asked during the soup course – a delicious lobster bisque.

'I always think one should travel abroad as often as possible. Broadens the mind, as they say. Although of course, wherever you travel, you take yourself with you.'

Alternatively, he'd turn a question around and redirect it at me.

'Do you attend many conferences or exhibitions in your line of trade, or do you operate on a one-to-one basis?' I asked as Herr Ehrlich served a succulent boeuf bourguignon.

'Wherever I travel, it's good to come home. The impermanence of travel is counterbalanced by the permanence of home. Where is your home, Gemma, when you're not plying your trade at St Bride's?'

Or else he'd answer not the question I'd asked but the one he'd rather I'd have asked.

'It's very generous of you to sponsor Frieda's education,' I remarked while Herr Ehrlich was out of the room, taking empty dishes to the kitchen. 'Is this part of a broader programme of philanthropy, or is it a one off, perhaps because of a prior relationship with her family?'

'One of the joys of being a successful businessman is that it empowers you to act on opportunities to help others.'

I wondered whether he'd ever considered a career in politics.

'But enough about me,' he said as Herr Ehrlich returned with our desserts: individual portions of a gleaming tiramisu in individual glass ramekins. The gold flakes sprinkled on their surface glittered beneath the flickering candlelight. 'Tell me about your role at St Bride's. I gather it's your first year in post. Then I'd love an update on the progress of the girls' business projects. I hope my talk the other day has inspired them to aim high.'

Feeling defeated, I gave up trying to extract information from him. As we drank our coffee I talked about how much I loved teaching at St Bride's, my fondness for the girls and for my colleagues, and my delight at living in such gorgeous accommodation, albeit temporarily curtailed while the bursar sought funding to repair my staff flat. I didn't like to ask outright for a donation, but I thought it wouldn't do any harm to make him aware of the situation, just in case he felt moved to stump up a contribution.

'Ah, Gemma, you have my sympathy. Living in a stately home has its trials as well as its blessings, as I know at first hand from living here at Torrid Manor. But fear not, I'm sure the girls will do you proud and through their business ventures, raise sufficient funds to fix your roof in no time.'

I tried to smile.

'If their ideas prove as profitable as they are imaginative, I may be lucky. Time will tell. Has Frieda told you yet about her brilliant idea for a sale of the girls' art?'

Mr Goldman-Coutts picked up a small, silver handbell that sat to the right of his wine glass. Its sound was so much more delicate than the brass one we used at school.

'No, but now would be the perfect time for her to do so. She and Rolf should have finished their meal by now – they were eating the same as we were – so I would like her to join us now and tell me all about it.'

Joining us a few moments later, while her father cleared our table and brought coffee, Frieda took a seat on one of a pair of stools either side of the fireplace. She chose the one closest to Mr Goldman-Coutts.

The girl's eyes sparkled with pride as she described to her sponsor how she had come up with the idea for the art sale, and I backed her up by telling him how enthusiastic her new friends were. Perhaps describing them as friends was slight exaggeration – Frieda still kept her distance to a certain extent – but I hoped it might encourage her to feel a closer connection with them too.

Her enthusiasm was infectious, and Mr Goldman-Coutts became almost as animated as she did during their conversation.

'I hope you will come to support our sale, sir,' she said. 'And maybe you bring some friends who like to buy art too?'

Here at last was a hint of what his business interests might be.

'Do I gather you are an art dealer?' I asked, feeling a little intrusive but realising time was running out to make any further enquiries of him in person.

He put his head on one side.

'Some might describe me that way. I had had some, er, dealings with galleries in Eastern Europe.'

I sat up straighter, looking at the paintings that hung either side of the fireplace.

'Are these part of your collection? May I look more closely?'

He nodded. 'Please help yourself.'

'Not that I know much about art,' I said as I got up from my chair and went to examine the picture that hung closest to Frieda. On a plain black background, dozens of childishly simple figures executed in a range of acid-bright colours were tumbling across the page, white dashes indicating their implied motion. It didn't look like great art to me, reminding me of jelly babies being shaken out of a packet. I wondered whether a valuable provenance might have earned it pride of place here in the dining room. I peered at the signature, hoping to find a familiar name. But it was illegible – in the candlelight, I could only see a little squiggle. I made what I hoped was an appreciative sound, albeit rather non-committal.

'I would love to see more of your collection if you have time?' I added.

Almost without thinking, I'd hit upon a good excuse to look at more of his house than this one room.

Mr Goldman-Coutts pursed his lips.

'I'm sorry, it is not possible at night. Only in daylight. The electricity, you see...' He waved a hand around. 'We are still waiting for much of the rewiring.'

Bother. I was getting desperate now.

'Then perhaps I might just visit the bathroom before we head off?'

This was something of a non sequitur but at least it gave me a reason to explore. The bathroom would probably be at least a few rooms away, perhaps down an interesting corridor where I might sneak a peek through a few doorways into other rooms without being caught, especially as Herr Ehrlich had now settled down by the fireplace, on the stool opposite Frieda's, where he was warming his hands before the flames.

Frieda stood up to whisper in my ear.

'I would not recommend the toilets here, Miss Lamb. I think you should wait until we are back at school, if you can.'

Her pleading expression persuaded me. If there was no indoor plumbing, I was not willing to venture out into the garden to use an earth closet.

Mr Goldman-Coutts coughed and glanced at his watch. Now that I was standing closer to him, I could tell it was genuinely expensive. Perhaps Oriana had known that all along and had just been trying to find fault with him, in return for his failure to notice her.

'Miss Lamb, is there a curfew at the school? Must you be back on duty by a particular time or find yourself locked out?'

'Don't worry, all the other girls will be tucked up in their dormitories by now, and my housemistress Oriana was doing the bedtime rounds tonight, so I'm off duty until breakfast time now. The school building was locked up by the bursar after our departure, but I'm to text a colleague on my way home to let us in again. If all else fails, or I can't get a mobile signal, I can shout to our night watchman, Max Security, or the bursar, who both live in lodge houses by the gates, to admit us. As a sixth-former, Frieda has her own room, so she will be able to creep back in and go to bed without waking her friends.'

When I mentioned Max, Mr Goldman-Coutts smirked and exchanged knowing glances with Herr Ehrlich. 'Max Security? Is that what he calls himself these days?'

Of course, we all knew that wasn't Max's real name, but it didn't make him any less effective in keeping us all safe.

'He's a very good security guard,' I insisted, only later that night wondering what Mr Goldman-Coutts meant by that question. Might he and Max be friends from a previous existence somewhere? Max had always cultivated an air of mystery about his career path before joining St Bride's, so I couldn't rule it out.

Our host began to drum his fingers gently on the table. 'Good, good. A high standard of security was one of the reasons we chose St Bride's for Frieda, of all the schools that might have been glad to take on an extra pupil in the middle of the academic year.'

I'd assumed he'd just chosen us because we were geographically closest to Torrid Manor.

'How handy that we're near neighbours too.'

I was pleasantly surprised to realise he'd chosen St Bride's on merit rather than for the sake of convenience.

'Ha, yes, quite so.'

I returned to my seat and drained my coffee cup, savouring the thick, dark liquid as it slid across my tongue – so much subtler than the staffroom brew I was used to.

'Anyway, we should really be heading back to school now, if you will excuse us, so as not to be tired in the morning. The school day is pretty action-packed, and Frieda will need her wits about her from breakfast time until supper, as will I.'

It was going to be hard to exchange the safety of this seat before the comforting, open fire for the perils of Herr Ehrlich's erratic driving through the cold, dark lanes back to my poky servants' quarters. Being Oliver's passenger would be so much more agreeable, but I was wary of offending either Herr Ehrlich or his employer by rejecting the chauffeur service.

'*Rolf, bitte fahren Sie Frau Lamb und Frieda nach Hause,*' he instructed. Rolf, please drive Miss Lamb and Frieda home. Then he glanced at me with an uncharacteristic nervousness. Perhaps it was because I hadn't heard him speak German before. His accent sounded native to me, compared to mine, at least, but perhaps he was wondering whether, as a teacher, I'd be judgmental about his grammar. I was flattered that he thought my German good enough to notice any errors.

I tried to spare his embarrassment by pretending not to have been listening to their exchange. I fiddled with one of the little dishes of snowdrops lined up along the centre of the table. I wondered who had picked them. There'd been no mention of any other resident. Was Herr Ehrlich Mr Goldman-Coutts' entire staff? The meal had been delicious. Perhaps he was actually a trained chef, and he'd only assumed the roles of chauffeur, gardener and PA temporarily as a favour to his employer while he recruited further employees.

Gently I tapped one of the little white flowers to make it nod on its impossibly slender stalk. 'These are so pretty.'

Mr Goldman-Coutts gave a fond smile.

'We have carpets of them in our grounds here. I understand that once they naturalise, they can multiply hugely.'

I nodded. 'My parents have some in their front garden at home, and there are quite a few in the school gardens too, although they're just about over now for the year.'

Mr Goldman-Coutts pushed back his chair and stretched his legs towards the fire, his face dappled by the flickering flames. He clicked his fingers at Herr Ehrlich.

'Yes, we've no shortage of snowdrops. Rolf, please fetch some paper to wrap some bunches of flowers for Frieda and Miss Lamb to take home. Frieda, I'm sure you would like some to decorate your bedroom, wouldn't you?'

Frieda nodded eagerly.

'I would like that very much, thank you. I shall draw some for you as a present. I am teaching myself to draw with pastels now.'

Mr Goldman-Coutts nodded in approval, and when he realised Rolf was still relaxing by the fire on his stool, he repeated the request in a rapid German that I couldn't follow.

'I must head back too now,' said Oliver as we awaited Rolf's return. 'The roads will be a joy to drive on at this time of night with virtually no traffic other than long-distance lorries, but it'll still take me a good ninety minutes to get home. Thank you so much for your kind hospitality, Sebastian, and for your patience with my questions. Frieda, it has been a pleasure to meet you too, and your father. I wish you the best of luck with your studies at St Bride's.'

Then he turned to me.

'Can I offer you a lift, Gemma?' he added. 'St Bride's School isn't far out of my way.'

'Both of us, you mean, Oliver.' I meant it as an instruction rather than a question. After the warmth of his greeting earlier, I didn't want to compromise myself by travelling home in the dark alone with him.

'My dear Oliver, please do not trouble yourself,' said Mr Goldman-Coutts. 'Your journey is long enough without needless detours. Besides, Rolf is expecting to take the ladies home. He won't have put the Rolls away yet.'

It seemed I had no choice in the matter.

Just then, Rolf returned with a recent copy of *The Times* and a few elastic bands. Rather clumsily, he broke a few stems as he wrapped two great bunches of snowdrops in the newspaper. He put one in Frieda's hands and kissed her on the cheek, before laying the final package beside my wineglass and stood to attention beside my chair. At least he didn't try to kiss me.

'*Schöne Edelweisse für die gnädige Frau,*' he said, with a little bow, clicking his heels together.

Beautiful edelweiss for the gracious lady. Edelweiss? Surely not!

I got to my feet, instinctively returning his bow, but in my haste, I pushed the heavy throne back too abruptly, badly stubbing Herr Ehrlich's right big toe.

'*Autsch, das tut mir verdammt weh,*' he cried, reminding me a German character in a Tintin cartoon strip.

Hastily, I pulled the chair back further away from his feet, and he swung round to sit on the newly vacated seat. Kicking off his right shoe, he revealed surprisingly luxurious socks. They must have been pure silk, their sheen reflecting in the candlelight. At the ankle, in ornate embroidery in the finest thread was a lavish, swirling letter C.

He raised his stockinged foot to his lap and clutched it with both hands, muttering gutturally under his breath.

'Pappi!' With a cry of alarm, Frieda dashed to his side and put her arms around him, murmuring comforting German phrases that I did not need to understand to realise how heartfelt they were. It was the strongest display of emotion I'd yet seen in the girl.

'My dear Rolf, how unfortunate,' Mr Goldman-Coutts was saying smoothly. 'I'm sure it was an accident. But perhaps you had better not drive the ladies home now. Your pain may make you hesitate when you need to press the brake. Please go bathe your foot immediately to stop any swelling.'

Herr Ehrlich gave his daughter a final hug, then hobbled towards the door, still grumbling.

'Gemma, I'm afraid I've had too much wine to drive you myself.

But Oliver, might we take you up on your earlier offer to escort Gemma and Frieda back to St Bride's?'

'But of course, it would be a pleasure.' Oliver got up from his throne and strolled the length of the table, on the fire side, to shake our host's hand. 'And I'll let you know as soon as my paper schedules your interview for publication. I can't promise a specific date, as that's out of my control, but please bear with me.'

Mr Goldman-Coutts' brow clouded for a moment.

'Oliver, you do promise you won't mention my address? This is my secret bolthole, you know. I couldn't bear to have my privacy invaded by paparazzi.'

So much for the prospect of a property makeover article. But Oliver concealed any disappointment with a warm smile.

'As I told you at the outset, it's the paper's policy to protect our subjects' privacy. Believe me, it won't be an issue.'

Personally, I thought Mr Goldman-Coutts was flattering himself if he thought photographers would be beating a path to his door. He seemed rather dull compared to the celebrities they usually targeted.

Our host nodded slowly. 'Good. I trust you, Oliver Goldsworthy. And remember that if you keep your word, not long from now, I will give you the biggest story of your career.'

Oliver's eyes widened, as did his smile.

With Frieda and I clutching our newspaper bundles, Oliver led us by the light of his phone across the hall with the Armada ceiling, into the entrance hall and out into the night.

While we'd been indoors, the moon had risen and the earlier clouds had dispersed, making it easier to navigate our way across the gravel than when we'd arrived. Oliver's sports car was parked in a shadowy corner of the forecourt. No wonder I'd missed seeing it when I was getting out of the Rolls-Royce, still traumatised by Herr

Ehrlich's reckless driving. When Oliver had opened the door of the Rolls-Royce to me, I had eyes only for him.

Now he opened the rear left passenger door and motioned to Frieda to get in. She did so.

Once he'd closed the door, while she was fastening her seat belt, he stood with his hand on the front passenger door and whispered to me before opening it.

'Stroke of luck, you mashing the poor chauffeur's toe, eh? Or did you do it on purpose to prevent him driving you home?'

'No, but I might have done if I'd thought of it. He is the most dangerous driver I've ever had the misfortune to be driven by. Which is alarming considering he's meant to be a professional chauffeur.'

'Perhaps he was the only applicant for the job.'

I grinned as he opened the door and allowed me to settle my bundle of flowers carefully on my lap before fastening my seat belt.

Finally, he got in himself, put the car into gear, switched on the headlights and entered the drive. As we passed through the square hole in the hedge, he slowed down, before braking in front of the wrought-iron gates.

'Blast. I'd forgotten about these gates. Ehrlich had to drive out to unlock them for me when I arrived earlier.' He turned off then engine. 'I suppose we'll have to do a U-turn and go back to the manor to ask Sebastian for the key.'

Just then, a light appeared behind us, flashing in the rear-view mirror. We turned round in our seats to see Mr Goldman-Coutts setting an electric bicycle on its kickstand. Then he strode towards us, holding out the big, cast-iron key Herr Ehrlich had used earlier. Oliver wound down his window to greet our host.

'Allow me,' said Mr Goldman-Coutts, before heading for the gates. He unlocked them and pulled them wide open, before giving us a little bow and gesturing to us to pass through. He and Herr

Ehrlich seemed to do a lot of bowing. I wondered if they were keen on karate.

Oliver turned his car key in his ignition and drove slowly through the open gates, before stopping to watch Mr Goldman-Coutts haul them closed, relock them and clamber back aboard his bicycle. We watched until his rear light had passed through the square hole in the hedge and he'd vanished into the darkness.

17

THE ROAD HOME

As we joined the public highway, Oliver broke the silence.

'It's just occurred to me that Sebastian wasn't wearing a crash helmet.'

'So? It's not compulsory for cyclists, only for motorcyclists.'

'Still reckless, though. That guy seems to like living dangerously. I'll put that in my article.'

As we turned onto the main road, I remembered I was meant to text Joe my arrival time so that he could unlock the front door for me. While I tapped a message into my phone, Oliver touched the screen on his dashboard to summon up some gentle background music.

Once I'd pressed 'send', I realised all was quiet in the back seat, apart from a very gentle snoring sound. I turned round to see Frieda had nodded off, her head slumped forward on her chest, her breathing slow and steady.

Perfect! Just what I needed to be able to speak in confidence to Oliver. All the same, I kept my voice to a confidential whisper to avoid disturbing her, and to allow me to hear if her sleepy breathing changed to wakefulness.

'So what did you manage to find out about Mr Goldman-Coutts' background and business interests? Anything juicy? Anything we should be worried about?'

'Well, Judith Gosling was right about the property. He has only just bought Torrid Manor, and the reason it's in such darkness is not because he's worried about his fuel bill, or because he's exceptionally environmentally aware, but because there's absolutely no mains electricity. There's just a small, diesel-powered generator in the kitchen to power essential electrical appliances such as phone chargers and laptops, boiling kettles, and running a microwave.'

'But we've just had a five-course meal! How does his chef manage with no mains power?'

Oliver laughed, in his mirth slapping the steering wheel with one hand.

'His chef? Which one, Mr Marks or Mr Spencer?'

I shook my head, puzzled.

'Gemma, have you not been food shopping in Marks and Spencer recently? We've just been served a fine selection from their top-of-the-range ready meal selection, many of which require no preparation beyond unboxing onto a plate or bowl and at most, a quick zap in the microwave. Trust me, as a self-catering bachelor without a culinary skill to my name, I can spot a ready meal a mile away, and tell you which supermarket it comes from and how much it costs. Not that I'm complaining. I'm lucky to be able to afford to live on them. But I'll tell you for sure: that mad German guy is the sum total of Sebastian's staff.'

'How extraordinary. I wonder whether is qualified to do any of his supposed jobs? I can cross chauffeur off the list after my experience earlier tonight, and gardener too. Did you hear him call these snowdrops edelweiss? No one who knew the slightest thing about gardening could confuse a snowdrop with an edelweiss.'

'Ha! I wonder what on earth Sebastian sees in him. Has Ehrlich got some kind of hold over him, like blackmail? What does he know about his boss that we don't?'

I bit a fingernail for a moment.

'I hope there's nothing that might compromise the school. If he turns out to be a criminal, other parents might withdraw their girls from St Bride's, fearing for their well-being.'

We were silent for a mile or two as we considered the possibilities, then Oliver spoke.

'Maybe Goldman-Coutts just couldn't find anyone else willing to work for him out here in the sticks in such a desolate, derelict house in the middle of winter. Maybe he offered to send Ehrlich's kid to private school to persuade them to take the job at all. Although the days are getting longer and lighter now, the nights are still jolly cold. It must be freezing in Torrid Manor once you step away from that open fire. Paying for Ehrlich's daughter to go to a posh school nearby would be a very persuasive perk.'

'A private school, with its small classes, might be better for Frieda too, as she's not a native English speaker,' I replied. 'She'd benefit from the extra attention.'

We paused at a crossroads.

'What's her behaviour like?' asked Oliver. 'Is it possible she's been expelled from state schools and can't find one to hold her? Did Dad find out when he registered her for St Bride's?'

'I think this is the first English school she's been to since she left her homeland, wherever that is. She refuses to speak about it.'

'Surely Caroline or Dad must know her nationality?'

I liked that he was calling the bursar 'Dad' already, despite having only discovered their relationship a few weeks before. I turned to look at him. His profile was disconcertingly similar to Oriana's, although the set of his neck and shoulders were the bursar's. The resemblance made me feel as if I'd known him much longer than a few weeks myself, for as long as I'd known the bursar. Admittedly, I'd only known the bursar since September, but in the closed, concentrated community of a boarding school, time seems to move at a different pace.

'Maybe he's just lived such a privileged life that state schools are off his radar,' I wondered aloud. 'Did you gather anything about his political leanings during your interview?'

'He wouldn't be drawn on politics. Although he did bang on a bit about freedom of speech, but then he went off at a tangent on freedom of expression in art, and on the question of repatriating works of art to their originating culture.'

'What, you mean the Elgin Marbles and that sort of thing? Tribal art brought back by colonial forces?'

'That's the ticket. Maybe he's been involved in brokering deals between governments and museums internationally. That's a hot topic right now. Hmm, I wonder if I could get a story out of him along those lines? That should be relatively easy to place with a national paper.'

'So, is that his trade? I suppose technically speaking, that could be described as import/export. If so, negotiations would be sensitive, so he might not want to speak openly about what he does for a living.'

'It doesn't sound like the sort of career that would buy him an Elizabethan country house in the Cotswolds, even a derelict one like Torrid Manor.'

He slowed down at the sight of a little muntjac deer standing uncertainly on the verge ahead. We lingered to allow it to cross the road unscathed.

'Actually, I wondered whether he might get his money from art dealing. He mentioned a connection with an art gallery in Berlin.

Perhaps he just provides the cash and doesn't get involved in their day-to-day operations.'

'Ah, hence his facility with German,' I said. 'Maybe he traded Herr Ehrlich for a painting at his Berlin gallery, as payment in kind.'

Oliver laughed.

'Whatever the painting, he was robbed!'

'Anyway, that explains why he gave such a dreadful speech when Hairnet invited him to inspire the girls to be entrepreneurs. He just bankrolls deals rather than being the brains behind them.'

Oliver slowed down to turn into the school drive, pulling over by the lodges because the gates were locked here too. Max padlocked them around suppertime every evening, just as the bursar would have locked and bolted the front door of the main school building, before leaving by the servants' entrance to return to his cottage for the evening.

As Oliver pulled on the handbrake, Max emerged from the shadows, key in hand, to release the padlock.

'How did you know it was me?' I asked. 'Even I wasn't expecting to be brought home in this car.'

Max tapped the side of his nose. 'Psychic powers.' He winked in greeting to Oliver and smiled at the sound of Frieda's snoring, which was now quite loud.

'Didn't you just text Joe your ETA, Gemma?' said Oliver. 'He probably messaged Max to open up for you.'

Max gave a rare smile. 'Rumbled. You stopping, Oliver?'

Oliver peered through the windscreen at the bursar's lodge.

'Actually, I'm going to look in on my dad while I'm here and grab a quick coffee and a catch-up before I head back to London. I did text him earlier to ask whether I might, and he said that would be fine.'

'That's nice,' I said to Oliver, meaning it. 'So, I could have cadged a lift off you anyway, even if I hadn't crippled poor Herr Ehrlich first?'

'I did offer earlier on if you remember. But Sebastian overruled me.'

'The bursar will unlock the gates again when you go,' said Max.

Leaving Max padlocking the gate behind us, we covered the winding drive at a much more sedate pace than my outward journey with Herr Ehrlich.

'Thanks very much for the lift, Oliver,' I added, as we came to a halt on the forecourt. 'Really useful debrief too, although I'm not sure we came to any significant conclusions.' As I leaned over to give him a grateful kiss on the cheek, he caught my hand.

'So, Joe's coming down to let you in, not Oriana? You and Joe...?' He broke off.

I smiled apologetically, not that I had anything really to apologise for. 'Yes, Joe and I are still an item. Sorry, Oliver.'

He gave my hand a little squeeze before he let it go.

'Oh, well, just thought I'd check. Lovely to see you, Gemma, and if I can find out any more about Lord Torrid there, I'll let you know straight away. To be honest, my current impression is that he's completely straight. I don't think you need to worry about him.'

'Are you really doing a newspaper feature on him, by the way?'

'God, no, that's just a cover. I don't think any of the editors I've worked for would have heard of him. I'll just have to string him along if he chases me up about it, and I'll keep an eye out for opportunities to place a piece somewhere. I'll check out niche art magazines. But I don't think he'd be bothered if it came to nothing on that score. What interested him more was befriending an independent journalist whom he could get on side for when he's ready to tell some story that's bubbling under. He told me before you arrived that it could be the scoop of my career.'

'Really? What kind of scoop?'

'He wouldn't be drawn.'

'I wouldn't get your hopes up too high, Oliver. It's possible that it's a non-story and he just underestimates how illustrious your career has been to date. Sorry, that sounded rude. No offence.'

He grinned. 'If he has, he wouldn't be far wrong. I've mostly spent my career reporting niche business stories and ghost-writing rich people's memoirs. But I am a competent reporter and writer, and I do have some half-decent contacts, so you never know. It could pay me to keep my options open with him. Anyway, look, there's Joe waiting at the door for you.' He pursed his lips. 'Don't let me keep you. And don't forget Sleeping Beauty in the back there either.'

I released my seatbelt and opened the door. Before climbing out, I scooped the newspaper parcel of snowdrops from my lap into my arms.

'Thanks again for the lift and the insights, Oliver. You're a pal.'

I set the flowers on the car roof for a moment while I opened the rear passenger door and gently touched Frieda on the shoulder.

'Come on, Frieda, we're back at school now. Out you get.'

She frowned in her sleep, then when I tapped her shoulder again, she opened her eyes, looked around as if trying to recognise where she was, remembered, and smiled.

'Thank you, Miss Lamb. Thank you, Mr Galsworthy. I have had a happy evening. Thank you.'

She passed me her parcel of flowers before unclipping her seatbelt, stepping out of the car and straightening up.

I gazed up at the building in front of me, illuminated by the motion-sensitive lights. After the gloom of Torrid Manor, the school seemed as bright as a seaside pier in high summer at full moon. But as to Goldman-Coutts' motivation, I was still pretty much in the dark.

'Safe journey home, Oliver. And have fun with your father.'

I closed the door and turned to wave to Joe. As we stepped lightly across the crunching gravel, I couldn't wait to tell him about my evening.

18

COCOA WITH JOE

'Good evening, Frieda,' said Joe. 'Good evening, Miss Lamb. Have you had a nice time?'

Frieda beamed. Still sleepy, she was very relaxed, no doubt partly still on a high from spending so much time with her father. I hoped her contented air would last now she was back at school.

'I have had a very happy evening, thank you, Mr Spryke,' she said, before yawning. 'But now I am very tired. I go to my room. Thank you for taking me, Miss Lamb.'

I wanted to send her to bed with a maternal hug, but held back. I didn't want to take inappropriate liberties, just because I'd had the privilege of spending an evening in the heart of her—her what, her family? Her home? I still wasn't sure.

As she headed off to her bedroom, she was humming quietly. Joe waited until she'd passed through the door at the end of the corridor before speaking again.

'So, Mr Moneybags didn't send you back in his Roller? If he's got a fancy sports car as well as the Phantom and the Harley-Davidson, Frieda's school fees must be like pocket money to him.'

Then he heaved the big front door closed, locked it, and pushed the bolts across before turning to give me a welcome hug, now that no one could witness our embrace.

Was he teasing me? Had he recognised Oliver's car and was about to take me to task for being out on a date with Oliver when I had said I'd be spending the evening having dinner with Mr Goldmann-Coutts? My ex had demonstrated a destructive jealousy on far flimsier evidence.

'Actually, I had a lift back from Oliver Galsworthy.' It felt good to be able to tell the truth without worrying about its impact on our relationship.

'Old Oliver Galsworthy? Where did he spring from? I didn't know he was down this way.'

'Mr Goldman-Coutts had invited him to dinner too.'

'Goodness, I had no idea they were connected. So, are they mates? Business associates? Was it Oliver who recommended St Bride's to him, rather than another pupil's parent?'

'Actually, no. Other way around. I emailed Oliver to ask him whether he knew anything about the mysterious Mr Goldman-Coutts through his work as a business journalist. He'd been unable to find anything out about our host from his usual sources, so he asked for an interview on the pretext of writing a profile piece about him for a Sunday newspaper. Next thing he knew, he had a dinner invitation, and to my surprise, he was at Torrid Manor when I got there. He had no more expected to see me than I did him.'

'Wow,' said Joe. 'Not a bad surprise though. Oliver's okay.'

I was glad Joe didn't seem to regard Oliver as competition. I decided to keep Oliver's parting comments a secret. After all, I'd made my preference for Joe perfectly clear to Oliver.

'Who else was there? Was it a big do?'

'Just me, Frieda and Oliver – oh, and Frieda's father, waiting on the table. And apparently doing all the cooking too.'

'He must be multi-talented. I wouldn't have put Herr Ehrlich down as a Renaissance man.'

I laughed. 'Believe me, he really isn't. I've never seen such a bad driver. I thought we were going to die on the way to Torrid Manor. Not that it bothered Frieda – she was too busy chatting to him the whole journey.'

'Really? Did you pick up any interesting gossip from their conversation?'

I wrinkled my nose.

'No such luck. They had the communication window closed the whole time. Couldn't hear a thing. Mind you, probably just as well because it meant they couldn't hear my squeals of alarm at his driving either. Now, come on, let's go down to the school kitchen for our cocoa. It's nearer than our flats and will probably be much warmer.' Unlike Lavender Flat, my room in the servants' quarters didn't have its own kitchenette or bathroom. Nor was it on the school's central heating network, but relied on tiny electric heaters that did no more than take off the chill. 'Then I can tell you all about my evening in comfort.'

We trudged down the lower stairs to the hub of the school's domestic operations. The huge, whitewashed kitchen was dominated by a couple of massive Agas and a vast, scrubbed, pine table serving as a central work surface. The room smelled faintly of bleach and dishwasher detergent, a remnant of the post-supper clean-up routine. I set my handbag and my newspaper bundle on the table before putting some milk to heat in a saucepan, then we sat down on ancient, pine chairs, their once-flat seats worn into little hollows by generations of bottoms. The table and chairs were likely the originals from when the property served as Lord Bunting's stately home.

'So how come Oliver drove you home instead of Herr Ehrlich?'

As I waited for the milk to heat, I spooned cocoa powder into two mugs, while regaling Joe with my description of Ehrlich's perilous driving habits. Joe alternately laughed and cringed at my ordeal.

'Thank goodness you got home in one piece!'

'Yes, I think if he asks anyone else to escort Frieda, we'd better advise them to drive themselves.'

When the milk on the saucepan began to emit a low rumble at simmering point, I returned to the stove and whisked it away from the ring before it could boil over.

'Fortunately, Frieda didn't seem at all perturbed by her father's driving. I suppose she must be used to it. Either that or she was just so pleased to see him that she didn't even notice it. It was rather touching how contented they were in each other's company. I was glad that Mr Goldman-Coutts allowed them private family time together. They only joined us at the end of the meal.'

I poured the hot milk onto the cocoa and set his mug on the table in front of him, before wrapping my hands round my own to benefit from its warmth.

'Hazel was telling me after supper tonight that she's desperate to get an invitation,' said Joe. 'She sees it as the opportunity to buttonhole him about her need for a new art studio.'

I raised my eyebrows. 'Good luck to her.'

'So, was Oliver down this way anyway or did he make a special trip? Don't tell me Hairnet's offered him a job?'

I perched on the table, resting my feet on the chair next to his.

'Not that I know of. And I don't suppose Oliver would be remotely interested in working at St Bride's, in any case. He likes his city life. Besides, his portfolio career of journalism and commissioned biographies means he needs to be where the action is, or rather, where his subjects are.'

Joe sat up straighter. 'So did you enjoy seeing Oliver in action tonight, probing his subject for gripping column centimetres?'

I gazed into my mug. 'Unfortunately, they'd finished the formal part of the interview before my arrival, so it was mostly chit-chat over supper. But on the drive home, Oliver told me the key points of interest.'

'Did Mr Moneybags know Oliver's connection with the school?'

'I'm not sure. Of course, it'll be apparent from his surname if and when his biography of Piers Galsworthy comes out. Apparently, he's got a meeting about Piers' biography with a publisher next month, but he says he'll run the manuscript past the bursar and Hairnet before it goes off for editing to make sure there's nothing in it that will embarrass them or harm the school's reputation.'

'So, it'll contain the truth, but not the whole truth?'

'Something like that. Still, it'll be better than no biography at all. I dislike biographers and memoirists that don't consider the finer feelings of others in their lives.'

Joe swirled the contents of his mug to combine them better, but I guessed he was really thinking about his former cycling team-mate's memoir that had caused him so much heartache.

'So what exactly did you find out about Goldman-Coutts? Was Judith right about Torrid Manor being tumbledown? Who else lives there with him?'

As we sipped our cocoa, I gave him as thorough a description of the evening as I could, saving the most amusing details until last.

'Then when Herr Ehrlich slipped off his shoe to nurse his stubbed toe, he revealed the most expensive-looking socks I've ever seen in my life. I reckon he's been stealing his master's socks.'

Joe threw back his head and laughed. 'What, you mean like Blackadder and Prince George, in that episode of *Blackadder the Third* when he's being pursued by murderous sock merchants wanting their bills paid? That's priceless. Maybe Ehrlich is more cunning than we give him credit for.'

I wrinkled my nose. 'I don't think so. He's a rotten impersonator.

For example, for someone who professes to be a gardener, he's a useless plantsman.' I unwrapped the newspaper bundle that I'd laid on the table to reveal the snowdrops Mr Goldman-Coutts had given me.

'He thought these were edelweiss.'

Joe held up one of the little bunches of white blooms to the light, admiring their fragility. The tiny blooms shone as brightly as if they'd been dipped in the kitchen's bleach bottle.

'Can't tell his amaryllis from his edelweiss, eh?'

'They're snowdrops, silly.'

'I know, but I thought it made a better joke. Anyway, I think we can rule out Austria as his homeland if he thinks its national flower looks like a snowdrop.'

Carefully, Joe picked up one of the delicate stems between thumb and forefinger and tucked it into my hair, behind my left ear.

I smiled and leaned down for a cocoa-scented kiss.

He gave a mischievous grin. 'Perhaps we should get Hairnet to invite Herr Ehrlich to talk to our budding entrepreneurs on how to blag your way into a job for which you're completely unqualified.'

'Or on how to be an opportunist. Oliver suggested Ehrlich might just have got the job because Mr Goldman-Coutts can't persuade any other staff to work in a near-derelict building. Full marks to Ehrlich for versatility, even if he is rubbish at driving and gardening. Fair play to him for getting Goldman-Coutts to pay Frieda's school fees. Ehrlich's living expenses must be pretty minimal now because his daughter's board and lodging are covered in term-time. Perhaps Mr Goldman-Coutts is not such a philanthropist as we've been crediting him for. He's simply self-serving.'

'But what is the man, exactly? Has Oliver been able to determine where he makes his money? Just what the nature of this import/export business is?'

I swallowed the remains of my cocoa.

'Yes, and that's the most interesting finding of the evening. We wondered whether he might be some kind of art dealer. So technically he's in import/export, although I reckon he's using that phrase to put everyone off the scent. Most people would assume it means he deals in manufactured or agricultural products, such as mass-produced clothing or tropical flowers. I think what he actually trades in is art. He is involved somehow with some Eastern European art galleries, although he didn't go into any specific details. I'm guessing that's where he first met the Ehrlichs and why he has a reasonable grasp of German. But he likes his privacy. Oliver says he's not listed as a director of any British business at Companies House, but he reckons that wouldn't preclude him from being in the international art trade.'

Joe took a moment to digest this information before speaking.

'Hazel would be the one to ask about this, but it strikes me that the elite art trade is pretty secretive. You know, with buyers hiding behind phone bidding at auctions, so no one knows where a piece of art is going to end up.'

He took our empty mugs to the sink and began to wash them up, along with the saucepan. I grabbed a tea towel from the overhead airing rack.

'So did he offer to show you his etchings?'

He wiggled his eyebrows suggestively. I laughed and flicked the tea towel playfully in his direction without doing him any harm.

'Nothing of the sort, don't worry. Although actually it's a bit odd, isn't it, that he didn't seem keen to show me any of his art collection? You'd think an art dealer would have loads of great pieces about his house that he'd show off to any visitor. He just made excuses.'

'I'll be relieved if he really is just an art dealer,' said Joe. 'I thought he was going to turn out to have a far dodgier background. Not that I wanted him to be a crook, for Frieda's sake as well as the school's. But for some reason, I assumed there was something illicit in his business dealings, judging by how evasive and non-specific his talk to the girls was.'

I finished drying the saucepan before revealing the juiciest news from my evening.

'Oh, but there may still be. As Oliver explained to me, top-flight, international art sales are notoriously suspect. You see, people can charge anything they like for a piece of art. It's not like a conventional commodity with a clearly definable value, like gold or oil or diamonds. Even though prices for minerals and fuel fluctuate, they only do so within a certain range; the value of art is entirely subjective. '

'That sounds like a brilliant way for two parties to pass the results of ill-gotten gains to each other under cover of a supposedly legitimate business transaction.'

'I know,' I replied. 'And it could have dire implications for the school, too, if we're found to be receiving ill-gotten gains, especially if Hairnet or the bursar know about it.'

'Surely they can't do? I thought the pair of them are as straight as they come.'

I reached my arms up around his neck for comfort.

'Me too. So, before we go making any accusations, we need to delve a little deeper.'

19

BUSINESS PLANS

Next morning, as I was enjoying a piping hot cup of coffee in the staffroom, I spotted on the staff noticeboard beside the pigeonholes a schedule in Felicity Button's neat hand. It showed dates allocated to business events run by the girls to showcase their new enterprises. All the girls had now chosen a theme for their business projects, ranging from dog biscuits to celebration cakes, from art to fashion.

'I hope this doesn't mean we're going to be forced to buy their wretched junk.' Mavis sighed as she dipped a shortbread finger into her coffee. 'I bet that's why Felicity's brought a plate of biscuits into the staffroom this morning: to butter us up. Look, there's a business card amongst them. Hardly subtle.'

Felicity was more supportive of the girls' strategy.

'Actually, I think that's smart marketing by our new young entrepreneurs running St Bride's Biscuits. They've even branded the paper plate with their new logo.'

She pointed to the pair of adjacent capital Bs, one the wrong way round, with a little circle floating above. 'See? B for Bride's, B for Biscuit, and a little halo to suggest the sainthood. Clever, eh?'

Mavis peered at it. 'More like the bulbous figure you'll turn into if you scoff too much of their product.' Her cynicism didn't stop her helping herself to another biscuit.

'The perfect loss leader,' added the bursar, coming to join us. 'Sound business practice. I take it those are the biscuits for humans, and not the dog variety?'

Mavis spluttered, spraying shortbread crumbs into her coffee.

Felicity laughed. 'Bursar, don't be so mean. I wouldn't feed you lot dog biscuits. Besides, the dog biscuits are shaped like cartoon bones, so you can't mistake them.'

Feeling a little sorry for Mavis, I diverted the conversation to allow her to enjoy the rest of her biscuit untroubled.

'Actually, loss leaders are a good idea. Why doesn't the school offer loss leaders, Bursar? Free sample days to potential pupils, in the hope that they'll love it so much here that they'll pester their parents into registering them for St Bride's?'

'Or put them off for life,' replied Mavis, recovering her usual form. 'Still, I might be persuaded to buy a few boxes of these short-bread fingers to top up the biscuit tin in my flat, if the price is right. They're jolly tasty. But don't get your hopes up, Bursar. I'm not buying enough to reroof the east wing. You'll have to reel in some punters with serious money if you want this nonsense to pay for the building works.'

The bursar stood up a little straighter. 'I'll have you know I'm not exactly standing idly by. Since half-term, I've applied for four different grants to try to get funding for the roof repairs, and although we can't expect instant results from those, at least we have a Plan B. Besides, you will be pleased to know, Miss Brook, that Miss Harnett, Felicity, Max and I had a very constructive meeting yesterday to draw up approved guest lists for all the girls' business events aimed at bringing in local spending power rather than relying on the school pound. I know we normally discourage visitors unrelated to the girls, but these events will be an exception, and Max will carefully monitor attendance for security purposes.'

Felicity backed him up.

'Yes, and because the school is so rarely open to the public, we're hoping the opportunity to step inside and admire our wonderful house and grounds will be an added attraction. Plus, of course we'll have a pile of the leaflets to hand, highlighting the importance of this historic piece of Cotswold heritage, hinting that donations for its upkeep for the benefit of future generations of locals are always welcome.'

'Have you got Mr Goldman-Coutts on your list for the sixth-formers' art sale?' I asked the bursar. 'I found out last night at his supper party that he's some kind of art dealer.'

Mavis guffawed.

'All the more reason not to invite him if he's used to the real thing. He'll be sorely disappointed by our girls' daubs. Better to focus on inviting neighbours with no taste, like that woman in Tetbury whose front garden is overrun by garden gnomes.'

'Ah, *les nains de jardin!*' crooned Nicolette. '*Les Anglais* bring them to France. Most French people do not like them, but to me they are what we call *des beaux laids* – lovely uglies.'

'I've met a few of those,' murmured Oriana on her way to her pigeonhole.

'Yes, but Mr Goldman-Coutts is both rich and philanthropic,' put in the bursar. 'So, he may well pay high prices for our girls' work, even if it's absolute rubbish.'

I smiled. 'Just as well that Torrid Manor's too dark to see what he puts on his walls. I found out last night that there's no mains electricity, so everything is illuminated by candles or firelight.'

'The perfect place to appreciate our girls' work,' said the bursar with a wry smile. 'I rest my case.'

I was glad Hazel wasn't there to hear the unfair aspersions cast on her girls' work, but I was also pleased that Mr Goldman-Coutts was on the guest list. The art sale could be the perfect opportunity for us to find out whether he really was an art dealer. If he made informed, intelligent comments about the girls' art, his claim would seem more plausible. But if he couldn't tell a bad piece from a good one, even at this level of art, we'd know he was hiding the true source of his vast wealth.

20

COURTING PEACOCKS

When I awoke next morning, lying in my narrow, hard, bed, I gazed up through the skylight. Judging from the quality of the light, spring was on its way at last. The sky was an almost Mediterranean blue, with not a wisp of cloud in sight. The promise of a proper spring day made me yearn to bunk off my lessons and spend the whole day roaming the school grounds and surrounding country lanes, patting lambs and spotting spring flowers. So when Hazel Taylor tapped on my classroom door during my free period mid-afternoon, I didn't need much persuading to abandon my marking and accompany her out into the afternoon sunshine, surprisingly warm for mid-March.

She slipped her arm through mine as we made a slow circuit of the rose garden, where the neatly clipped bushes were just starting to put out tiny, lime-green leaf buds.

'I want to pick your brains, Miss Lamb.'

'What about?'

'Mr Goldman-Coutts. I'm just wondering whether you gathered any indication of the kind of art he likes. If he's an art dealer, he's more likely than any of the other girls' fathers to buy art that isn't their own daughter's work. If I know his tastes, I can advise the girls to include in the art exhibition whatever he's most likely to buy. So did you pick up any clues? Should I go for, say, bucolic landscapes and naturalistic portraits, or Damian Hirst style spot paintings? There's no point in putting up paintings that pay homage to Van Gogh and Monet if what he really craves is a modernist colour block. It would be jolly handy if he did prefer the latter. I know that as an art teacher I shouldn't really say this, but the girls could easily knock out a few Mondrian look-alikes to order.'

'Bit harder if he'd rather have a few Gainsboroughs,' I said. 'Although I'd be impressed if you have any girls who can produce a fair imitation of those, especially at such short notice. Your exhibition's next week, isn't it?'

'Actually, I was rather hoping you'd tell me Torrid Manor's walls are adorned with modernist monochromes. Did you notice any Yves Kleins or Gerhard Richters?'

Although I had never heard of either of those artists, I began to feel more optimistic about the roof repair fund.

Reaching the far corner of the rose garden, we took the straight path dissecting the lawn and headed for the old, walled garden, once the kitchen garden supplying all the fruit and vegetables required by Lord Bunting's household. These days, the only productive part of the garden in terms of edibles was the array of espaliered fruit trees ranged against the high, red-brick walls. The beds, divided by a grid of gravelled paths, were now given over to low-maintenance shrubs.

We passed between low, grey bushes stripped of almost all their leaves. Relieved of the weight of their foliage, the bare stalks stuck up straight, as if surprised by a recent ambush. I pointed at them with a wry smile.

'I'm guessing one contingent of girls has set itself up to make lavender bags or essential oils.'

Reaching the stone seat at the centre of the north wall, we rested for a few minutes, basking with upturned faces and closed eyes, the spring sunshine warming our faces. Our backs and bottoms were heated too, the stone bench having absorbed and retained the sun's heat like a natural storage heater.

'For two pins, I'd take forty winks just now,' remarked Hazel. 'That's a pin for every twenty winks. What a bargain. I'd even settle for twenty winks. The prospect of this art sale is taking it out of me, even though theoretically, it's the girls doing all the real work.'

I sat back and stretched out my legs.

'This little break will do us both good. I'm glad you suggested it. I feel like a poster girl for the benefits of vitamin D.'

I spread my arms and my fingers to absorb every possible drop.

'Anyway, to answer your question, I'm afraid I have no idea about Mr Goldman-Coutts' taste in art. Apart from the dining room, the rest of the house was pitch-dark. I could barely see the black outlines of picture frames on the walls as we passed through the Great Hall, never mind the actual pictures. I did my best to get him to show me his art collection, but he said that would only be possible in daylight as they're still waiting for the electricians to rewire the house. Honestly, I don't know how anyone can live like that, especially at this time of year while the days are still quite short and before the clocks have moved to British Summer Time.'

'So was there any art on display in the dining room where you said you had the firelight and candelabras for illumination?'

I thought for a moment.

'Only a pair of pictures that were a kind of pop-art, I think. You know, the sort that have little outlines of people dancing about, looking like animated jelly babies. Andy Warhol, is it? One of his type?'

Hazel guffawed. 'Do you mean Keith Haring?'

She pulled out her phone, tapped in a quick search, and held up the resulting image to show me.

I beamed. 'Yes, that's the one. Though I couldn't see a proper signature, only a little squiggle in the corner. We were sitting in candlelight, and the fire was alongside the picture, so didn't add much illumination.'

'Shame. It would have been worth a fortune if it was a Haring original.'

'Oh, it looked like an original. It wasn't a print. I could see the brush strokes.'

Hazel's lips twitched at the corners.

'I don't suppose I'll ever look at one his pieces without salivating for jelly babies now.'

I laughed.

'Sorry about that. But do you think—'

Just then, a raucous shriek from the stone pavilion adjacent to the walled garden made us both jump. I clutched Hazel's arm in horror.

'Whatever was that noise?' I cried, my heart thumping in fright. 'It sounded like a girl being strangled.'

We both leapt to our feet and ran down the diagonal path to the pavilion, ready for whatever action it took to protect our girls.

The shriek came again, followed by a chorus of giggles that did much to put our minds at rest. In its wake came the mellifluous tones of a violin being played very, very well. After a few notes, I recognised the tune – a lilting modern ballad that had recently spent some weeks at the top of the charts, making number one on Valentine's Day.

The violin playing continued, interrupted by the occasional, nerve-jangling squawk, which, now we were closer to it, we realised was animal rather than human and strangely familiar.

'Oh, Hazel, how daft are we?' I declared. 'Isn't that just the sound of a peacock?'

Reassuringly, there was another burst of laughter.

'Actually, they just sound like they're having fun, but we'd better investigate anyway, to make sure,' said Hazel.

We slowed to a walking pace. I don't know about Hazel, but I was beginning to realise we'd overreacted.

'That can only be Grace in Year 11,' observed Hazel. 'She plays exquisitely, but not usually out of doors.'

'Perhaps she's taken to busking. Now there's a business idea for the more musical girls.'

'With talent like that, Grace might make a fortune busking in Tetbury at a weekend, or in Cirencester on market day. Well, some money, anyway, in return for nothing more than her time and the effort to get there.'

'With any luck, she might turn out to be like the chap in the Sherlock Holmes short story, 'The Man with the Twisted Lip', who finds he can earn more as a beggar than plying his official trade as a journalist. He wasn't any ordinary beggar, I recall, but an experienced actor who knew just what to say to make people cough up.'

We followed the music like Hamelin's children in the wake of the Pied Piper.

As we entered the pavilion, we were almost knocked off our feet by a barrelling bundle of feathers: a large, male peacock scurrying in our direction, defiantly sounding an alarm in his breed's distinctive voice.

'I thought that was its mating cry?' said Hazel. 'Yet he seems to be fleeing from the peahen the girls have got lined up for him there.'

'We're thinking he might prefer classical music,' said a plaintive voice, which I recognised as belonging to one of the youngest girls.

A little huddle of Year 7s was clustered around the peahen, who was allowing them to stroke her head and neck, stepping back and forth between them.

Hazel bent to pat the peahen's head in sympathy. 'What are you expecting to get out of this: the peacock's fancy tailfeathers?'

Although the autumn moult had long been collected by the girls, spectacular new feathers had been growing during the winter, ready for the spring breeding season. I'd recently spotted a sixth-former sporting drop-earrings framing the eyes cut from tail feathers with silver wire. I hoped the girls wouldn't be tempted to pull out the fresh growth before it was ready to fall.

'No, Miss, we would never be that cruel,' said Imogen. 'We're just trying to persuade the peacocks to breed, so that we can sell their eggs to hatch as pets.'

I bit back a smile. 'And you thought a little romantic music might get them in the mood?'

The girls nodded earnestly. 'Well, it could only help.'

'What about you, Grace?' I asked. 'Surely you had the sense to know that wouldn't work?'

The violinist lowered her violin from her chin as she shot me a knowing look.

'Yes, of course, Miss Lamb. But these kids asked me. This is a business engagement for me. It's earning me money. I don't like to turn down a business opportunity.' She swapped her bow to her other hand, gripping it along with the neck of her violin, then slipped her free hand into her jacket pocket. She fished out a hand-made business card scattered with musical notes and treble clefs.

I read the text aloud. 'Fiddler on the Hoof. Music on the move. £10 per hour.'

She swapped her bow back to her right hand and pointed it at the peahen's admirers.

'That's £2.50 you owe me, kids. Cash on delivery, no cheques or bank transfers.'

Rosalie handed over a handful of coins.

'I suppose Miss Bliss would tell us to put this down in our cost of sale column,' she said.

'We can probably set it down against tax too,' said Zara. 'So, it's not all bad news.'

'Such a shame it didn't work,' said Angela. 'I bet peacocks' eggs are really pretty if their tails are anything to go by.'

'You'll have to ask Dr Fleming about that, but it doesn't follow,' advised Hazel. 'Duck eggs are pale blue, for example, and I've never seen a pale blue duck.'

'Actually, the peahens are the ones that lay the eggs,' I added gently. 'They're the females of the species. The peacocks are the males.'

Assured that both girls and birds were safe, Hazel and I began to stroll back towards the stable block.

'Still, full marks for initiative,' remarked Hazel, as we entered the classroom courtyard. 'Even though Dr Fleming would be unimpressed by their knowledge of peacock biology. Oh well, I suppose I'll just have to encourage my art students to put a mix of work into their exhibition, something to suit all tastes. I just hope for the sake of the girls' egos that someone buys a piece of work by each of the young artists.'

'Call me selfish,' I replied, 'but for the sake of my flat, so do I.'

21

SPECIAL GUESTS

In my opinion, the sixth-formers' art sale the following week was likely to be the best potential money-spinner of all the events set up to showcase the girls' enterprises. Given my vested interest in its profitability, I'd done all in my power to make it a success, poring over proof after proof of the exhibition catalogue, compiled during sixth form English classes to hone the girls' persuasive writing skills.

'Try to make visitors want to buy your picture from the power of your prose alone, regardless of the quality of the artwork,' I'd told them, hoping the pictures would be worth buying without any persuasive words at all. I'd only been to the art studio once or twice, but I'd seen plenty of the girls' paintings displayed around the rest of the school. They were certainly expressive of the girls' individuality and there were a few I was particularly fond of, although I was not qualified to judge their quality or market value.

The catalogue was to be anonymised to protect the privacy of each artist – a classic St Bride's safeguarding measure as well as a means of discouraging vanity or jealousy. Quite a few of St Bride's pupils were the daughters of famous people in various spheres, from high financiers to film stars, from landed gentry to leading industrialists. A few of them were simply famous for being famous. Hairnet and Hazel rightly did not want visitors to purchase pieces simply because they were created by famous people's children – and then put them up on eBay (or eBeach, as Hairnet called it), to make a handsome profit for themselves.

This rule applied to all the girls' enterprises. They were allowed, however, to adopt a name for their business and to develop a brand logo. As well as the St Bride's Biscuits and Grace's Fiddler on the Hoof, there was a home-baked dog biscuit business called Fido's Favourites, a celebration cake company called the Cakesters, and a fashion makeover service called Fashion Sesame whose logo showed a genie emerging from an Aladdin-style lamp.

As the artists were individuals rather than joint ventures, Hairnet had allowed them to develop stylised monograms as their branding. She suggested as their role model the cyphers designed for King Charles III and the Queen Consort.

As I'd helped so much with the catalogue, Hairnet asked me to join Hazel in supervising the event. My contribution would be to tick off the guests on a check list as they arrived in the entrance hall and hand them an exhibition catalogue before passing them to a member of the sixth form who would escort them to the art studio. Once all the guests had arrived, I was allowed to visit the exhibition myself and mingle with our visitors.

Max would also be posted in the art studio. On any occasion when outsiders were invited onto the school premises, he was on hand for security duties.

Half an hour before the guests were due to arrive, I popped over to the art studio to see how the exhibition looked, so that if anyone asked me about it while I was on door duty, I could give the right answers. The display showed a variety, in terms of media, theme, originality and competence. True to the St Bride's spirit, all the young artists seemed to have been allowed to express their own personalities and interests. I wasn't sure they'd all be snapped up by buyers, although purchasing a piece to support the school didn't oblige them to display it in their homes.

But it was good to see the girls all working together as a team, putting the finishing touches to the displays, admiring each other's work and giggling in excited anticipation at the imminent arrival of their guests. Even Frieda seemed more engaged than usual with the other sixth-formers. Perhaps having something practical to work on together had made it easier for her to interact with her peers, rather than having to rely on conversation and banter in a non-native language. I was glad she seemed to be settling in at last.

Now she led a little delegation towards me.

'Miss Lamb, do you like our exhibition?' she asked, her eyes sparkling. 'Do you think we have done well? I think it is good. I think we will make lots of money today.'

I smiled at the little crowd of eager artists.

'Yes, Frieda, you and your friends have done very well. Now, I must return to my post to welcome your guests. I'll do my best to butter them up for you, I promise, so by the time they reach the exhibition, they'll be eager to spend.'

Frieda's face fell. 'Butter up? Why the butter?'

The others laughed, but not unkindly.

'Come with me, Frieda, I'll explain,' Sylvie was saying as I left. 'Then you can teach us another funny phrase in German.'

'*Ja wohl!*' cried Frieda, and they all giggled together.

As I waited in the entrance hall for the first guests to arrive, I cast my eye down the guest list, wondering whether there'd be anyone I knew besides the girls' families and, of course, Mr Goldman-Coutts. I was pleased to see Herr Ehrlich's name there. For once, he was to visit the school in his role as Frieda's father, rather than as his employer's chauffeur.

I was just puzzling over a series of other Germanic names – surely there wasn't a German quarter of the Cotswolds that I didn't know about? – when a familiar friendly voice calling, 'Hello, Gemma!' distracted me from my clipboard.

It was Sophie Sayers, hand in hand with her other half, Hector Munro. Together, they ran the Hector's House bookshop and tearoom in Wendlebury Barrow, our nearest village. Joe and I often went there for afternoon tea in our free time.

'Sophie, Hector, hello! How nice to see you!'

'What fun to have an excuse to see you on your home turf for a change,' said Sophie.

'We're looking forward to seeing the art studio too,' added Hector.

I was happy for the school to tap wealthy people for money, but I knew Hector's House was a low-profit business, and I felt uncomfortable at putting pressure on my less monied friends.

I lowered my voice. 'Don't feel obliged to buy anything, by the way.'

'To be honest, the walls of my cottage are already so full of the pictures that my great-aunt collected on her travels that I don't think I could fit any more in,' said Sophie. 'Hector's flat is more minimalist. No pressure, Hector!'

She winked at me.

'I think you mean tidy,' Hector corrected her. 'That's not to say I wouldn't mind the odd new picture if I can find one that suits my style.'

'And we've empty wall space in the tearoom,' added Sophie. 'We've been thinking of offering it as a selling gallery space to local artists, for pieces that would look right there. With a reasonable margin added for the shop, of course.'

'That would be fabulous,' I replied. 'When you get to the art studio, have a word about that idea with our head of art, Hazel

Taylor. The bursar will be over there too, if you need to talk about the financial side of things.'

Sophie turned to Hector.

'It'll also send a subliminal message that the shop is endorsed by a prestigious public school,' she told him. 'And vice versa. Though we should probably display some pictures from the village school children and the local comprehensive, for balance.'

'Sounds good to me,' I said, certain that the bursar would welcome the regular stream of income from that route, no matter how tiny. 'Anyway, let me pass you over to one of the girls, who will give you a catalogue and be your guide.'

Hector had a twinkle in his eye. 'So the girls' parents pay you to put them to work earning money for the school? Are you sending them up chimneys too?'

Hector was still grinning as I introduced them to their guide, the next free girl in the waiting queue of sixth-formers.

The art exhibition was due to last for two hours, but within the first twenty minutes, everyone but Mr Goldman-Coutts, Herr Ehrlich and the mysterious German quartet had arrived. It was such a good turn-out that all the sixth form guides had been used up, some of them returning several times to escort a fresh set of visitors to the art studio. Now I was alone in the entrance hall, awaiting the latecomers.

To my surprise, they all turned up at once, and they appeared already to know each other. As they came through the door, they were chattering away in German in a similar accent to Herr Ehrlich's. I assumed he must have family to stay. If Mr Goldman-Coutts was allowing all four of these burly men to stay at Torrid Manor, he was an even more indulgent employer than I'd given him credit for.

Seeing me with my pen poised over my clipboard, Mr Goldman-Coutts came over to me straight away, oozing his usual charm.

'Miss Lamb, I'm so sorry we are late. I had fully intended to be here on the dot of two o'clock, but an unfortunate minor incident on the road delayed us.'

Before I could stop myself, I glanced at Herr Ehrlich, who was looking at his shoes.

'That's one advantage of my choice of car. The Rolls rebounds very well. Not a scratch on her.'

I couldn't help wondering how the other vehicle involved had come out of the event – or animal or, God forbid, a pedestrian. But Mr Goldman-Coutts was keeping the details to himself.

The four men resembled each other: tall, broad, and hirsute, with raven hair and chocolate-brown eyes beneath bushy eyebrows – rather like Herr Ehrlich, in fact. Not similar enough to be blood relatives, but possibly fellow countrymen.

Herr Ehrlich raised his eyes to me and gave his odd little bow.

'Frau Lamb, *einen schönen guten Tag*.'

'*Guten Tag, Herr Ehrlich, willkommen*.' I gave an encouraging smile to make it clear I held no grudges about his perilous driving from the other night. Having exhausted my conversational German skills, or at least my confidence (I could understand a lot more than I could speak), I continued in a clear, slow English. 'How nice to see you. I hope your toe has recovered.' I pointed to his foot, raising my eyebrows in enquiry, and he nodded and smiled. 'Have you brought your family?' I indicated the group of four, who were standing a few paces behind him, perusing exhibition catalogues. 'Are these your brothers or cousins perhaps? You are so alike.'

Herr Ehrlich turned to his party and translated what I had said. Then they laughed as if he'd just told them the most uproarious joke. One of them slapped his thighs and another clapped his hand on his friend's shoulder as if to stop him collapsing to the ground in mirth.

'*Ach, nein*,' replied Herr Ehrlich, turning back to me. 'But they are friends who like the art. Mr Goldman-Coutts asked Frau Harnett to bring these friends and *die gnädige Frau*, she say yes.'

In his thick, guttural accent, he pronounced his employer's name as 'Goltman-Kurtz', making me think of the sinister Kurtz in Joseph Conrad's *Heart of Darkness* and his cry of 'The horror! The horror!'

Perhaps he was hoping to lift his daughter's spirits by providing guaranteed buyers for her art. I didn't like to tell him that hers would be indistinguishable from the other girls' work. Unless, of course, she'd let him in on the secret of her identifying monogram. Not that it mattered if she had – those codes were there to fox guests not otherwise associated with the school, such as Sophie and Hector, rather than family members.

'Well, they are very welcome,' I replied, meaning it. The men's suits looked expensive – perhaps the Swiss equivalent of Savile Row. I hoped they had deep pockets, too, metaphorically speaking. Between them, they might boost the roof repair fund nicely. For a moment, I allowed myself to imagine moving back into my flat, the roof repaired and the rooms redecorated.

22

BIDDING WAR

'As you're the last of our guests to arrive, I'm allowed to leave my post now to escort you across.'

'We're honoured,' replied the ever-chivalrous Mr Goldman-Coutts.

I closed the front door and bolted it for security, knowing Joe's PE lessons that afternoon would be indoors in the gym, rather than on the playing fields at the front of the school.

As I led the way through the corridors, the Germanic gentlemen chattered among themselves in their own language. Able only to understand the odd word or phrase, I was puzzled by their behaviour on our way to the classroom courtyard. Occasionally they stopped to examine a framed oil painting from Lord Bunting's legacy on the wall. One of them produced a jeweller's loupe from his pocket and held it against an exquisite wooden doorframe carved with vine leaves and bunches of grapes. Their manner reminded me of very fussy house-hunters, expecting to find dry rot or rising damp at every turn. I wondered if Mr Goldman-Coutts was thinking of expanding his local property holding and these gentlemen were surveyors checking the places for woodworm.

Either that or for listening devices. That idea almost made me laugh aloud.

'Sorry, gentlemen, the house is not for sale.' I tried to sound jocular, but I was unnerved by their interest in the fabric of the building. What on earth were they looking for?

It was a relief to leave the main building and go out into the open air to the classroom courtyard. As we climbed the wrought-iron, spiral staircase to the art studio above the classrooms, the buzz of lively conversation floated down to us through the open windows. When we entered the studio, it was clear that the visitors were enjoying the event, tea and cake in hand as they chatted animatedly to their sixth form hosts.

As my party began to tour the exhibits, I looked for red 'sold' dots on the girls' pictures and was gratified to see quite a few. I hoped the buyers had paid decent prices, not just token payments to salve their conscience for eating so much cake.

As soon as Hairnet spotted Mr Goldman-Coutts and his entourage, she cut through the chattering throng to welcome them.

'My dear, I was starting to think you weren't coming.' That seemed a little rude by her usually high standard of etiquette, but Mr Goldman-Coutts didn't seem in the least offended.

He leaned down to speak confidentially, his dark eyes twinkling. 'I can't say I wasn't worried myself.' He glanced surreptitiously at Herr Ehrlich, perhaps as a hint as to who was to blame for their delay.

Perhaps a little flustered by the presence of so many strangers in our usually isolated enclave, Hairnet dipped a curtsey to Herr Ehrlich, before gathering her wits and shaking hands with Mr Goldman-Coutts' entire group. Fortunately, at that moment, Frieda materialised and dragged her father away from the little huddle for a hug and a chat – a welcome diversion from Hairnet's embarrassment.

'Now, gentlemen, don't let me keep you,' Hairnet continued. 'You will want to make up for lost time before the best pictures are snapped up. All excellent in their own way, of course. Beauty in the eye of the beholder, ha ha.'

As the gang of six began a methodical circuit of the exhibits, the other guests parted to make way for them, withdrawing to the centre of the room to continue their conversations. Presumably they'd already earmarked their purchases and wanted to make the most of the local networking opportunities – and of the abundant tea and cake. Many of the guests knew each other. Cotswold society is a small world.

As I turned to speak to Sophie and Hector, who were tucking into flapjacks with their tea, Max marched over to the German party and greeted the four newcomers like long-lost friends. I'd never seen him so chatty, and all in a foreign language too.

Without obviously eavesdropping, I strained my ears, hoping to catch at least the gist of their conversation. Did Max really know them, or was he just seeking to practice his German? It seemed he spoke it fluently, which I'd never known before. But then, why should I have done? I'd never seen him in Frieda's company before, apart from when she was asleep in Oliver's car, and she was the only native German speaker in the school. I guessed now that was why he had been chatting to Herr Ehrlich on the forecourt the day Frieda first came to the school. He must have been embracing the opportunity to practice his excellent language skills.

'Something wrong, Gemma?' asked Sophie, noticing my attention straying.

'Sorry, how rude of me, Sophie.' I turned my back to the little group, not wanting to arouse suspicion.

'Did you see the pair of beautiful paintings one of the girls has produced of old, leather-bound books?' Hector was saying. 'I presume she must have used some old books from the remains of

Lord Bunting's collection in the school library as her model. Those pictures would be just right for Hector's House, so we've bought both of them for the shop.'

'Come and have a look, Gemma,' added Sophie.

I followed her across the room to admire their purchases. By chance they were displayed right next to where the German party were now poring over a set of pen and ink sketches that paled in comparison beside these bright, vivid oils.

'Oh yes, they're lovely,' I said. 'Those vibrant colours would show up really well against the pale walls of your tea-room.'

'I'm hoping they'll serve as a subtle advertisement for our second-hand section in the flat above the main shop,' said Hector. 'Not that I think we have any old books that look quite that glossy, although we do have some that are leatherbound. We polish them now and again to nourish the leather. Perhaps we should be doing that more often.'

'*Bitte sorgen Sie sich nicht, niemand hier spricht Deutsch, außer der kleinen Prinzessin,*' Max was saying. '*Die Frau Lamb spricht nur ein bisschen. Im Krise, könnten Sie "Feuer!" oder "Hilfe" schreien.*'

Please don't worry, I translated in my head. *No one here speaks German apart from the little princess. Miss Lamb speaks only a little. That doesn't matter. In a crisis, she could shriek 'fire' or 'help'.*

As they all laughed, I saw Max glance at me, then look quickly away, his smile fading. I hoped he was embarrassed when he realised they were talking disrespectfully. Hairnet would have had a fit if she'd realised how patronising Max was being towards poor Frieda. The girl might be a bit stand-offish but calling her 'a little princess' was unfair. She might not have been the most approachable girl in the school, but she didn't exactly give herself airs and graces.

'We haven't decided yet whether to put them up for sale or to keep them,' Hector was saying. 'I also bought an unusual black and white ink drawing of a pile of burning books that I thought I'd hang in my flat. An unusual topic for a schoolgirl to choose, but a powerful reminder of the dangers of censorship and fascism. Or have you just been studying Ray Bradbury's *Fahrenheit 451* with them?'

Before I could answer, a sixth-former sidled up to join us.

'I just heard you talking about my paintings of the old books,' she said proudly. 'I can paint you more to order if you like. I'd give you a good price.'

I suppressed a smile at her wheeler-dealing. 'Ten out of ten for opportunism, Katya,' I said, 'but remember, no one's meant to know who painted what until after the show's over.'

She gave a guilty grin. 'Does it really matter now, Miss Lamb? All my pictures have been sold now anyway, so I'm happy. Besides, I think the buyers here will enjoy our paintings all the more if they know they've met the artist. Here.' She reached into her skirt pocket and pulled out one of her home-made business card, featuring a lavish K monogram in silver ink and her business name, Pages Portraits.

Sophie took it from her and showed it to Hector, who nodded his approval.

'Thank you, Katya,' said Sophie. 'We'll bear your kind offer in mind.'

Meanwhile, Mr Goldman-Coutts and friends were crowded around Hazel Taylor.

'I'm so sorry, any pictures with red dots on have already been sold to our earlier arrivals,' Hazel was saying. It seemed odd that he didn't know that from his own art galleries. 'But if you wish, I can ask the artist responsible to produce new ones in the same style.

Mr Goldman-Coutts' right eyebrow began to twitch.

'*Unmöglich*,' he murmured. '*Unglaublich*.' Impossible. Unbelievable. But to Hazel, he said, 'No matter. My friends would like to buy the rest of this artist's work on display here, and when you see how much they will pay for each piece, you will regret selling cheaply to the first bidder that came along.'

Hazel paled.

'I'm so sorry, Mr Goldman-Coutts, but the invitation card did make clear that this was to be a straight sale, not an auction. If something is sold, it is sold. But I'm sure the artist will be thrilled by your generosity and appreciation of her hard work. She drew those pictures in her own time, in her room, you know. They're quite different from the more colourful, lively pieces she has been producing in my art lessons.'

Mr Goldman-Coutts translated for his henchmen, and for some unknown reason, they laughed.

Fortunately, further embarrassment was averted by a sudden interruption – the scrabbling of tiny claws scampering across the laminate floor from the door to the far end of the room. Not far behind came a feline wailing, then McPhee, not usually so energetic, leapt in from the landing at the top of the spiral stairs to pursue a small creature across the floor.

Immediately, there followed the sound of human footsteps pounding up the spiral staircase. Olga, a Russian girl in Year 10, stood in the doorway, raising her hands in the air to express her desperation.

'Help! Help! My business assets have escaped!'

The room fell silent, apart from the yowling in the far corner. The girl scampered across towards the cat, who was crouched under a table, tail like a bottlebrush, deciding whether to pounce on his prey. Without a thought for Hairnet's finer feelings, Olga grabbed McPhee's tail in both hands and pulled him out into the open. He dug his claws into the floorboards, creating deep scratches in the parquet and filling the air with a sound as grating as fingernails scraping down a blackboard.

As Olga scooped him up in her arms, McPhee turned round to face her, yowling again, and reaching up his right front paw to fend her off.

'Ow! You little beast!' The scratch on her cheek began to ooze scarlet blood. As she turned her face away from him, her stray business asset, a large, brown rat, saw its chance to escape, darting past her and weaving its way between any visitors' feet that blocked its way to the door. Abandoning his German friends, Max darted after it, while McPhee, yowling with indignation, leapt out of the Olga's arms, landed on all fours, sped towards the door and rattled down the metal stairs and out of sight.

Open-mouthed, Hairnet froze at the centre of the now silent room, her hands on her hips. Then she must have remembered her audience, whose attention was now on her.

She closed her mouth, forced a smile and clasped her hands in front of her chest.

'Now, who's for any more of this delicious cake?'

23

THE RAT AND THE CAT

That evening, immediately before supper, Hairnet took the unusual step of calling a whole-school meeting. In financial terms, the sale had gone well, judging by the bursar's face. He had flushed pink with pleasure when, after the last guest had departed, Hazel showed him the total taken on the girls' summary sheet. But now Hairnet looked ashen.

For this impromptu meeting, there'd been no time to put chairs out down the sides of the hall, so the staff stood at the back.

'Girls, I am sorry to disrupt your evening, but something dreadful has occurred,' she began. 'I am also sorry to have to share such bad news. My beloved McPhee has disappeared, following an unfortunate incident at the art exhibition this afternoon, and he has not come in for his supper.'

A hand shot up in the front row, where the youngest girls sat on the floor cross-legged.

'Did someone buy him by mistake? Was he sitting so still that someone thought he was a sculpture?'

Hairnet took her question more seriously than perhaps it deserved.

'My dear, he was far from stationary at the art exhibition. In fact, I have never seen him move so fast as when he chased what I have learned is Olga's pet rat across the floor.'

That caused a stir.

'Olga's got a pet rat in school?'

'Not fair!'

'How come she gets to have her rat at school and I can't bring my pony?'

Hairnet waited for the inevitable flurry of questions to die down, before beckoning towards the centre of the room, where Olga's year group was sitting.

'Olga did not have permission to bring her pet to school,' said Hairnet. 'The school rules forbid the import of pets. And I use the word import advisedly because Olga, where did the pet rat come from?'

Olga stood up and made her way to the front of the assembly hall to stand beside Hairnet. Hairnet nodded to her to explain her side of the story.

'Vladimir came back with me from Petersburg in my suitcase.' She spoke loudly and clearly, as if giving evidence in a court of law, the rounded tones of her Russian accent level and dispassionate. 'He travelled in my suitcase. He was comfortable in the little bed I made for him, and I gave him a water bottle in case he woke up on the journey. He did not suffer.'

Hairnet laid a hand on the girl's arm.

'In case he woke up? Is he a particularly sound sleeper, this Vladimir of yours?'

Olga shrugged. 'When I give him my father's sleeping pill, *da*. His wife, not so much.'

Hairnet's eyes widened. 'His wife?'

'Well, they have not had a wedding, but it is an exclusive relationship. Vladimir and Lyudmila, they are monogamous.' Olga's

English was really coming on well. 'Lyudmila, she woke up and ate some of my money. You see, they were in the suitcase that I bring the cash in for my fees. But don't worry, they were fine.'

'So that's why Olga's fees were a little short this term,' murmured the bursar, standing beside me. 'I thought her father had just used a less favourable exchange rate.'

'And did Mr and Mrs Rat have pet passports?'

Although Hairnet's voice was calm, her dread of the answer was clear on her face.

'*Nyet*, but if you would like them to have passports, I will ask my father to get some from the Dominican Republic, like he did for me. You see, it makes it easier to travel.'

The bursar turned to Frieda. 'That's a coincidence; that's where your passport is from too, isn't it?'

Frieda nodded.

'Yes, it is a good place to get a passport. You see, Olga, we are passport twins!'

Olga laughed and came over to give her a hug.

'Never mind this passport malarkey,' said Mavis, standing on my other side. 'I don't suppose the pesky creatures have been vaccinated for rabies. It's endemic on mainland Europe.'

'So where is Vladimir's wife now, Olga?' Hairnet was asking.

'I think Lyudmila has gone to find him.'

Hairnet cleared her throat and put her fingers to her lips for a moment.

'So, girls, what I must ask you all is to search your dorms and your sitting rooms and your bathrooms tonight for two large, brown rats. I will ask Mr Security to search the classrooms on his rounds tonight.'

A girl at the centre of the room raised her hand.

'What should we do if we find them, Miss Harnett?'

'Catch them by the tail,' suggested her neighbour. 'I think rats like being picked up by their tails.'

'No, you're thinking of mice,' said another.

'No, monkeys. They have infantile tails, haven't they, Dr Fleming?'

She turned to search for the science teacher among the staff at the back of the hall.

Dr Fleming's lips twitched in amusement.

'Prehensile, Sylvie. You're thinking of prehensile tails.'

Hairnet raised her hand for silence.

'Capture the creatures as best you can without touching them, and certainly do not let them bite you.'

Mavis snorted, then tried to turn the sound into a cough. 'Easier said than done.'

'Equally, if you have any sightings of the rodents, but cannot catch them, please report the details to Mr Security, who will take the appropriate action.'

'What's that?' murmured Mavis. 'Leg it? Stand on a chair?'

'Send them to live on a farm,' whispered Joe from behind me. 'I wonder how many of the girls would fall for that one? A special rat farm that will give them lots of country walks and treats.'

'Meanwhile, I am hopeful that McPhee will return to me of his own volition when he has recovered from his trauma. But if you see him, please pick him up and bring him to me. He will be somewhat easier to catch than Mr and Mrs Rat, being so fond of his cuddles.' Her voice broke for a moment.

'Miss, miss!' At the front of the hall, Imogen waved her hand in the air for attention. 'Can me and my business partners have the job of finding Olga's rats and McPhee? You and Olga can be the first customers for our new pet detective agency, Fluff Finders.'

Hairnet hesitated, doubtless keen to have as many children as possible searching for her beloved pet and his alarming new enemies.

'We offer a no-find, no-fee service,' wheedled Imogen.

Hairnet considered.

'You may all search, for the sake of efficiency, but only the members of Fluff Finders will receive a fee if successful.' She began to rally a little. 'Of course, if anyone else finds them, they may choose to sell them onto the Fluff Finders team at a lower price than their fee, so that they all benefit. Bursar, I think there is a business term for such an arrangement?'

The bursar blinked in surprise. 'Franchising?' he suggested uncertainly. 'Pyramid selling?'

It seemed the meeting was done.

'Olga, you may rejoin your friends,' said Hairnet. 'Now, off you go to your supper, my dears, and let's hope that tomorrow Olga and I are reunited with our special friends. But Olga, if and when your rats are found, I am afraid we must keep them in isolation for the safety of us all, and we will have to inform the authorities.'

Olga frowned. 'But, Miss Harnett, that's not fair. I was going to breed babies to sell as my business.'

Usually unflappable, Hairnet staggered a little.

'But how did you know we would be setting up businesses this term? We did not know ourselves until you were on your way back to school.'

Olga waved a hand dismissively. 'Oh, I did not know. I just brought them with me as pets from our dacha. But rats are quick to breed, you know, so it seemed an easy option.'

'So are nits, but that doesn't mean we want them multiplying at St Bride's,' murmured Dr Fleming.

Olga shrugged.

'Oh well, if we do not find them, there are plenty more on our dacha. I can easily get more when I go home at the end of term.'

'Now, run along.' Hairnet wiggled her fingers at the assembled girls. 'And happy hunting.'

All the girls got to their feet and headed for the Trough, except for Imogen, Rosalie, Zara and Veronica, who were kneeling in a circle at the front of the room, their hands pressed together, eyes closed and their lips moving silently.

I marched over to round them up. They were on my dining table, and school etiquette dictated that none of the girls on any table could start eating until all of its occupants were present.

'Come along, girls, what are you up to?'

Imogen opened one eye, while the others continued their antics.

'Sorry, Miss Lamb, we're just setting to work for our first customers with a prayer to St Anthony.'

I supposed it couldn't do any harm.

24

ON THE RUN

The girls seemed chirpy enough at supper, with the Fluff Finders team bright-eyed with optimism about their first case. But later in the evening, when I went to supervise their bedtime, they were distinctly downcast, and the reason was no mystery.

'Where do you think McPhee is now, Miss?' Imogen's voice was faltering. 'Do you think he's still chasing Vladimir, wherever he is?'

Knowing it would be easier to get them settled for the night if they were in good spirits, I took a positive approach.

'I expect he's gone home to bed himself by now, worn out by all that excitement. He's probably curled up fast asleep on Miss Harnett's bed as we speak.'

I hoped that cosy image might cheer her up, but instead her eyes filled with tears.

'You don't know that, Miss Lamb,' said Ayesha. 'It depends how far he chased him. Maybe Olga's rats are homing rats, like pigeons, and they're leading him all the way to Russia.'

'They like cats on boats,' said Zara. 'Precisely because they keep down rats and mice. My gran's got a book about a ship's cat. I bet they'd love having McPhee on a Channel ferry. They'd probably let him on even without a ticket.'

Imogen threw herself face down on her bed and sobbed. I went to perch on the edge of her bed and laid a comforting hand on her shoulder.

'Don't listen to them, Imogen; I'm sure there's no such thing as homing rats. Besides, why would they want to go that far, when St Bride's grounds are so huge and so beautiful? There's plenty of room for Vladimir and Lyudmila to play chase without heading further afield. They'd probably turn round when they got to the main road anyway. McPhee certainly would. We know McPhee doesn't like loud noises, and he'd stay well away from cars. Besides, they'll have got hungry by now. They'll probably have returned to where they usually eat – to Miss Harnett's flat for McPhee, and Vladimir and Lyudmila to Olga's bedroom.' I had been making this up as I went along, but now I was beginning to get into my stride. 'After all, that's how animals first became domesticated – by finding humans who will provide them with food and a comfy bed in return for their companionship. Far easier than having to search out food and shelter for themselves night and day.'

'Not if you're McPhee,' came a voice from the opposite bed. 'He'd just need to catch up with Vladmir and...' Isobel gnashed her teeth together to demonstrate. 'Free range rat for tea.'

'Or else Vladimir could ambush McPhee by turning round and taking a bite out of him,' said Cecilia.

'Or Lyudmila could gang up with Vladimir and attack from the other side, cornering McPhee. What was it Mrs Gosling called it when she was talking about the Battle of Hastings in our history lesson today? The lobster lunge?'

'Pincer movement,' replied Veronica, putting her fingertips to her thumbs and picking up her teddy bear by the ears.

I thought fast to try to keep ahead of these girls' vivid imaginations.

'I'm not sure rats are sufficiently sophisticated to organise a military campaign. Besides, we don't know that Lyudmila is on the loose too. I didn't see her in the art studio earlier, only Vladimir. In which case, he might have got bored by now with being out and about. He probably decided he was missing her and went back to his cage to have supper with her.'

I was glad Dr Fleming wasn't there to witness my outlandish take on rat behaviour.

'Or he might have gone home to mate with her.' Veronica nodded sagely. 'Well, that'll please Olga, because it'll increase her business assets.'

'Although if McPhee does pounce on him and kill him, she could still use him as a business asset but in a different way,' said Angela. 'You see, my grandad goes fishing, and he told me that at the place where he buys his bait from, they always have a dead rat in the back of the shop to make sure they've got plenty of fresh maggots. Olga could set up a business selling maggots to fishermen down by the lake.'

I quailed slightly.

'Now, I think that's enough talk about rats for tonight, girls, or you'll all be having nightmares.' I was a little worried I might too. 'Chances are, McPhee and the rats are all fine, so let's forget about them until the morning, shall we? So, into bed, quick sharp, please, or we'll have not time before lights out for the next chapter of *Doctor Dolittle*.'

Imogen gave a loud sob.

'But the thing is, we can't forget about them, Miss. They're on our conscience.'

'Nonsense,' I replied, starting to lose patience. 'It's no good trying to find them until tomorrow when it's light. You'll never find them in the dark. Besides, Mr Security will be patrolling the grounds as usual with his torch tonight, so he may well find them for you. It'll be so much easier to search in daylight tomorrow, and you can persuade your friends to help you. You can hire them as extra detectives, Imogen. What useful work experience that will be!'

'But it's all our fault,' wailed Rosalie.

'If it's anyone's fault there's a rat on the loose in school, it's Olga's, for breaking school rules and smuggling a pair of them here in her suitcase.'

'No, Miss Lamb, you don't understand. There are two of them on the loose. Lyudmila's out too. You see, Olga was keeping them in her sock drawer in her wardrobe.'

'Well, that's very naughty of her, but I suppose as long as she kept the doors closed, they'd be safely contained.'

'She did, miss,' Zara sniffed. 'But we sneaked in when she was in the toilet and opened her wardrobe and let them out.'

'You did what? Whatever for?'

'Well, the bursar had been talking to us earlier about what makes a good business, and he told us that the best businesses are oppor... oppotty... make opportunities for themselves. So we let out Olga's rats so that she'd need to call Fluff Finders to help her find them again.'

All four Fluff Finders bellowed their advertising slogan, developed in our English lesson that morning: 'Who you gonna call? Fluff Finders!'

I closed my eyes to let all this sink in.

'Well, girls,' I said at last, 'perhaps before we have our bedtime story, the Fluff Finders might like to try calling on St Anthony once more.'

25

POST-MODERNIST MAYHEM

The mood in the staffroom next morning was a little cheerier. Hazel had posted a sign on the noticeboard announcing the total takings from the art sale. It was a comfortable five-figure sum.

Nicolette gazed at the total. 'But we have only thirty sixth-formers. How many pictures did they make? They must have been very busy.'

I scratched my head.

'That's strange. There weren't that many pieces – no more than half a dozen per girl. The ones I saw sold were going for about £20 each – a generous enough sum, although less so when you consider how much tea and cake some of our guests consumed. I'm sure that antique dealer in oxblood corduroy trousers ate about forty quid's worth of fruitcake on his own.'

'Ha, I've seen him skulking outside the baker's in Tetbury too,' said Mavis. 'Greedy pig. Maybe he was filling his pockets.'

'He had a French pastry in each hand when I saw him,' added Hazel. 'I was worried he might leave sticky fingerprints on the girls' work. Honestly, you'd think an antiques dealer would have more respect for art.'

'I bet most of the guests weren't coming with the intent of offloading a pile of cash on our poor darlings,' said Mavis. 'They just welcomed the excuse to have a good nose inside our sacred walls, counting their twenty quid buys as entry tickets.'

'Hang on there.' Oriana raised her hands to silence us. 'You don't need a maths teacher to point out to you that thirty girls times six paintings times twenty quid does not five figures make.'

'It makes less than four grand, actually,' said the bursar. 'But what Hazel hasn't told you is that some of the pictures were bought for over a thousand pounds apiece. Quite a few of them by Mr Goldman-Coutts and his party.'

I frowned, puzzled. 'That's a very generous donation to our roof fund, especially when he needs to spend so much to make his own house habitable.'

'Actually, the four fellows he was with were stumping up a lot of cash too. And I mean cash. Great wads of £50 notes.'

'Really? But they don't have any vested interest in helping St Bride's, do they? Not like Mr Goldman-Coutts, who at least has a girl here by proxy, even if not his own daughter.'

The bursar shrugged. 'With any luck, they may all have daughters at home coming up to school age, and they're hoping to increase their chances of being awarded scholarships by helping us out in our hour of need. Anyway, ours is not to reason why. I'm off now to bank the cash before anyone changes their minds.'

'Have you got one of those pens that enables you to check whether bank notes are forgeries?' Mavis called after him as he headed for the door.

When he turned to stare at her, he looked pale, but didn't answer.

'Of course, the other possibility is that we have a genuinely gifted young artist in our midst and Mr Goldman-Coutts' friends are all art connoisseurs able to spot embryonic talent,' said Hazel brightly. 'If so, I'm surprised I hadn't already identified her myself.'

'I very much doubt that,' said Oriana briskly. 'When I saw them leaving the school later, I thought they looked like a load of culture-less oiks hoping smart suits will pass for class.'

'So, were those top-priced paintings all by the same girl?' I asked Hazel.

Hazel frowned. 'Well, that's what's so strange, Gemma. They were all submitted by Frieda, who said they were pieces she'd done in her own time in her room.' The sixth form had single rooms rather than sharing dorms. 'But the paintings she produced during art classes didn't attract a single buyer. They're in completely different styles, admittedly. She's been experimenting in pastels in lessons and, to be honest, she has yet to master the medium. The ones that sold were all her pen and ink drawings, astonishingly vivid for something monochrome, and rather angry. But I wouldn't have called them great art. Competent, technically, but not the work of a young prodigy.'

Oriana put her finger on the calendar pinned to the noticeboard.

'How many weeks has Frieda been at St Bride's?'

As her housemistress as well as her art teacher, Hazel didn't need to think about that. 'Four and a bit. She arrived the first day back after half-term.'

'And how many pen and ink drawings has she produced in that time?'

'Let me consult the catalogue. I'm not so familiar with those as I haven't seen her working on them.' Hazel flipped though the brochure, counting under her breath. 'Eleven. Blimey. A regular little Picasso in terms of productivity at least.'

'And Picasso didn't have a full academic timetable to contend with at the same time,' I observed. This was starting to sound fishy, but I held my tongue, not wanting to stir up trouble if there was an innocent explanation.

'But I'm guessing that Frieda had told her father and his friends what her monogram was beforehand, and they just looked for anything that was hers. Nothing to do with talent. They were just supporting her.'

Hazel nodded.

'You may be right. Mr Goldman-Coutts and his friends may have come expressly to buy all her work. They didn't pay much attention to anyone else's. And did you see, Gemma, how tetchy he and his chums were when they discovered that one of her pen and ink drawings had been sold before they arrived? One of burning books, apparently.'

'I wish I'd seen that picture,' said Mavis. 'I might have bought it to hang in my flat to cheer me up after a hard day's slog in the school library.'

I laughed. 'Hector Munro from the bookshop bought it for twenty quid, he told me. But he might be open to offers, Mavis, if you ask him nicely. If you like, I'll tell him you're interested next time I go there for afternoon tea. Or you could just commission Frieda to draw another one. She ought to be pleased that her work is in such demand.'

Hazel sighed. 'Well, good luck to you on that. But please tell Hector not to tell anyone what a bargain he got. And none of you are to tell the girls what each picture fetched either. We don't want a nasty outbreak of comparisonitis. I don't want to foster any jealousy that might drive a wedge between Frieda and her classmates. The poor girl's had a difficult enough time as it is. So, the official story is this: the sale was a great success, and each piece of art sold for about the same price. Now it's back to business as usual.'

'Yes, Miss Taylor,' Mavis, Joe, Oriana and I chorused in mock meekness. I was beginning to wish I'd bought one of Frieda's pictures for £20 myself.

26

FINDERS KEEPERS

With McPhee and the rats still missing, I decided to sacrifice my morning break to searching the gardens, along with the Fluff Finders and their new recruits. The clear blue sky and cold, bright spring sunshine were additional lures, and a healthy alternative to the fug of the staffroom coffee machine.

Since my leisurely stroll by the lake with Joe, more spring bulbs had opened up, and the leaf buds on the trees were now big enough to create a green haze about the branches when viewed from afar.

As the Fluff Finders spread out across the lawns and rose garden, with their new recruits heading for the walled garden and pavilion, I volunteered to circuit the lake.

I was pretty sure McPhee never pestered the ducks, but would a rat attack them? Could rats even swim? I suspected so. But then so could foxes. Presumably the prospect of a dip in a chilly lake to reach them in their cute little duck house was too big a price to pay, when they might find food elsewhere on dry land. All the same, I was glad to see the ducks were out in full force. The Fluff Finders would be distraught if they came across a pile of bloody feathers in their search.

A flash of reddish-grey fur glimpsed from the corner of my eye made my heart beat faster, but when I turned my head I saw only a squirrel darting up an oak tree.

Unhindered by any cloud cover, the sun was casting its spell on every little detail in the garden. Water droplets on the backs of the ducks clambering out of the lake sparkled like diamonds. Crocuses dotted about the emerald lawn glowed like glossy clementines in a Christmas fruit bowl. The bright light exaggerated the details of the lichens adorning the branches of trees, making them look like miniature worlds in themselves.

'As kingfishers catch fire,' I quoted aloud, making a mental note to find a space in the Year 11 curriculum for a discussion of the poems of Gerard Manley Hopkins, peerless celebrant of the natural world, finding the glory of God in all things.

But what could this be, sparkling like silver, in the acid-green grass in front of me? Surely nothing but silver itself. Silver was a natural element, of course, but it wasn't this smooth and neat when found in nature. This piece was gleaming like a highly-polished pebble. When I was at primary school, we used to sing a hymn that began, 'Daisies are our silver, Buttercups our gold'. But this silver disc was no daisy.

I stooped to part the grass, already starting to grow, but it had not yet had its first cut of the season. Sparkling beneath the matte-green blades lay a large, oval locket about the size of the top joint of my thumb, strung on a fine, serpentine, silver chain. In the clear light, a mesh of teeny scratches criss-crossed the polished metal casing, showing it was well worn and possibly antique, but the lack of tarnish suggested its owner had cared for it well.

I picked it up and turned it over in my hand. The surface that had been face up, catching the sun's rays and my attention, was the back of the locket: the part that lay flat against the wearer's chest.

Now I saw the front, embellished with a single letter, a capital C, in an old-fashioned, copperplate script, all curves and curlicues.

I tried to recall all the girls in the school whose names began with a C: Clara, Celia, Christina. The owner must be missing it very much and be anxious to be reunited with it.

What lay inside would likely provide a clue – a photo of the girl's parents or siblings or even of their pets. I may not yet have met all the girls' families or furry friends in person, but if the locket's owner was in my house, St Clare's, I might recognise them from the photographs the girls tended to pin above their beds.

When I slid my thumbnail beneath the little catch at the right-hand side of the oval rim, the locket popped open with the faintest of clicks. I parted its sides as far as the delicate hinge would allow.

Beneath a wafer-thin, glass disc curled a tiny lock of auburn hair, and facing it, a coloured photograph, neatly trimmed to fit the frame. It featured a woman of about forty, whose hair matched the sample opposite. She was gazing at the camera as if weighed down by the cares of a nation – a female Atlas straining beneath her burden.

What little I could see of her clothing looked foreign to me, reminiscent of an Eastern European national costume. The high-necked, full-sleeved, white blouse with an open neckline hung with tassels was embroidered in reds, golds and greens. Wherever she came from, she was proud of her origin.

I turned the locket over in the palm of my hand, gazing at the curly C, with its elaborate scrolls at top and bottom – as elaborate as the small size would allow, that is. Of course, it might not have been lost by one of the girls. They weren't allowed to wear jewellery with their uniforms, although I knew some of them did, keeping it tucked out of sight to avoid being told off. Maybe it belonged to a member of staff? Could the C be for Miss Caroline Harnett? I was sure I had seen it somewhere recently, or the monogram at least.

Something at the back of my mind was jarring, in the way it does when you spot an acquaintance outside their usual context and for a few seconds, you can't place them: your dentist in a museum, perhaps, or the supermarket checkout assistant walking her dog in the park.

I began to stroll across the lawn towards the classroom court-yard, conscious that the end-of-break bell would soon ring. In the distance, Imogen was pulling up her socks, which to my surprise made me remember Herr Ehrlich's ankles. Or rather, the mono-grammed silk socks I'd glimpsed by the light of Torrid Manor's open fire after I'd hurt his poor toe. The socks I'd assumed he'd borrowed or stolen from his employer, as they were far too luxu-rious for someone on a gardener's wages. If it was a Coutts family emblem, did it mean Mr Goldman-Coutts had a daughter or other relative at the school that we didn't know about?

Hearing the bell ring for the end of break, and in the absence of pockets in my sweater dress, I fastened the locket carefully around my neck, tucked it inside my collar out of sight, and headed for my classroom for the next lesson.

It wasn't until lunchtime that I had time to consider the matter further. Arriving at my classroom with ten minutes to spare before the first lesson of the afternoon, I popped into Judith's classroom, hoping to find her at her desk. One of Judith's hobbies was calligra-phy, so I thought she might be interested in seeing a finely-engraved monogram on a locket – and she might recognise who it belonged to.

As I entered her room, where she was poring over her next lesson plan, I undid the clasp and gently laid the locket in front of her.

'I don't suppose you recognise this necklace, do you?' I perched on the edge of the nearest pupil's desk.

Judith lowered her reading glasses, then picked the locket up and took it to the window to examine it in better light.

'I just found it in the grass near the lake,' I explained. 'I was looking for the missing animals, but got distracted by this little trinket sparkling in the sunshine.'

'It's more than a trinket, Gemma. I'd say it's a very fine piece of work. Possibly a family heirloom. How on earth did engravers manage to create such fine lines in the days before lasers?'

'Whichever girl lost it must be pretty keen to be reunited with it,' I remarked, swinging my legs like one of the girls. 'I can't understand why she hasn't reported it missing and asked everyone to look for it.'

Judith laughed. 'Now there's a business opportunity – the Silver Seekers, a sister company to Fluff Finders.' She flipped it open. 'Wow, what a striking, proud woman – and what gorgeous hair. It's like copper thread.' She looked up. 'I don't think we've currently got any girls with hair like that. Not that this woman's daughter would necessarily have the same colouring as her mother, but I'm guessing this is the mother of one of our girls.'

As she snapped the locket shut, she frowned in thought. Gazing at its front cover, her eyes widened in sudden recognition.

'Hang on, there's a tiny coronet above the C.' She pointed with the tip of her little fingernail. 'You don't notice it at first because it almost blends in with the ornate surround, but it's definitely a coronet.'

'I suppose that rules out Hairnet as its owner, unless there's something she's not telling us.'

She smiled. 'Yes, I think so. And what's more, I think I know where I've seen it before. It's like the monogram of one of the sixth-formers on their artwork. I looked around the art studio before the sale started, and I noticed it then. I wondered which one of the girls was giving themselves airs and graces making up such a pretentious cipher, but I didn't think any more of it.'

'Whoever it was, surely she couldn't have had this locket engraved to match her monogram design? Even if she had the locket already, when would she have had the time or the opportunity to take it to a jeweller?'

'It would have to be a very fine craftsman, too, not just any old high street jeweller,' said Judith. 'But I don't believe it's a recent engraving in any case. Look, you can see the centre of the design has worn away a little, in a way that could only happen with decades of use, an infinitesimal layer being removed every time one opened or closed the locket.' She peered more closely. 'Actually, I don't think this is a swirly C at all. I think it's an E with the cross-stroke worn away.'

A knock at the door alerted us to the arrival of the girls ready for the next lesson. Judith dropped the locket into my outstretched hand, and I closed my fingers tightly around it.

'My best advice is to take it up to the art studio and show it to Hazel. I bet she'll tell you at once whose monogram it is. That'll save you a lot of hassle. Mind you, it'll also dob up that person as a plagiarist for having copied their supposedly original monogram off an old piece of jewellery.'

'Never mind. I expect they'll prefer the embarrassment of being rumbled to losing this pretty locket forever,' I said, weaving my way through the tide of incoming girls to return to my own classroom.

27

IN THE ART STUDIO

As Judith advised, after my last lesson of the afternoon, I climbed the spiral staircase from the classroom courtyard to seek out Hazel in the art studio. The long room was filled with late-afternoon sunshine streaming through the dormer windows, providing the copious natural light that fitted it so well for its purpose.

Hazel was nowhere to be seen, but to my surprise, Max was in the far corner examining a pastel sketch of snowdrops that I recognised from her earlier description as the work of Frieda Ehrlich. He jumped as I greeted him, apparently oblivious that I'd entered the room. Although chuffed to have startled our security guard, I was also concerned that he was not at his usual high level of alert. What on earth could be distracting him up here?

'Hi, Max. I didn't have you down as an art afficionado,' I said lightly, hoping to put him at his ease. 'At least, not until I saw you chatting up our Mr Goldman-Coutts' art dealer friends the other day.'

He dropped the pastel sketch back onto the table and shuffled a few other pieces of art on the table as if hoping to disguise which picture he'd been examining.

'Me? Art?' He forced a laugh. 'Oh no. Routine patrol.'

He strolled over to meet me in the middle of the room.

'Still looking for those escaped rats?' I asked. 'I hate the thought of a couple of rats loose on the estate.'

He raised his eyebrows. 'More than two rats on site if you know where to look, especially at night. Many more. Nocturnal beasts.'

I shuddered. 'Well, I'm in no hurry to find any, regardless of their nationality. Although given a choice, I'd rather meet British ones than those smuggled in from a country where rabies is endemic. I hope you find them soon. And McPhee too, of course. Fingers crossed he hasn't caught anything from them.'

Max waved a hand dismissively. 'McPhee will be fine. All kinds of boltholes where he can lie low.'

'A bit like you, then, Max?' I joked.

He grinned. 'McPhee likes a nap in my tunnels. A hundred doting girls can get too much. But the Russian rats are sorted. Grabbed my night vision goggles and my dart gun. McPhee led me to them. Cornered them in an old glasshouse. Too smart to go in after them himself. Floor was covered in shattered glass.'

'Ouch!' I replied in sympathy. 'I guess a few kilos of well-fed cat would be more vulnerable to cuts than a rat. With its tiny paws and lightweight body, it might scamper across unharmed.'

'Yep. But the cat had the last laugh.' He mimed firing a gun. 'Single shot. One each. Stone dead. Took them to the vet in Tetbury. There they remain.'

I frowned. 'What was the point of that? Surely the vet couldn't revive them?'

'Course not. Rabies test. Results this afternoon. But caged pets are unlikely to have been infected. Still, must err on the side of caution. Anti-rabies jabs are no fun.' When he grimaced, I guessed he'd experienced one at some point in his mysterious past.

My relief was short lived.

'But hang on, Max, if there are so many rats on the estate, how do you know they're Olga's rats that you shot?'

'Red silk ribbons round their tails and scarlet painted claws. Very patriotic.'

'Did you manage to catch McPhee at the same time?'

He shook his head. 'Nope. Bolted at the first shot. But he looked fine. I told Hairnet he's safe. Stopped her worrying.'

'So why has no one told the girls to stop searching for them?'

'Useful practice for Fluff Finders, says Hairnet. Teamwork, lateral thinking and planning. She's not wrong.'

He wandered over to a table on which lay an array of pastel landscapes, a current art A Level project.

'Does anyone apart from Hairnet know you've taken care of the rats?'

He bent down to peer at the bottom right-hand corner of a black and white line drawing, the spot where the girls had been instructed to place their monograms.

'The bursar. That's all. So stay shtum, Gemma until Hairnet gives the all-clear.'

I wondered why he was telling me.

When he picked up one of the pastel drawings to examine in more closely, for a moment I thought he was about to tuck it under his arm and make off with it.

'Thinking of investing, Max?' I said lightly. I'd never known him take an interest in the girls' art before. At the recent sale, he seemed more interested in practising his German with Mr Goldman-Coutts' dealers than examining the exhibits. 'If so, I think you've missed the boat on the best deals. Hazel was saying in the staffroom this morning that some of the paintings were fetching a thousand pounds a throw. Or rather, some black-and white sketches – I think they were in pen and ink. Mr Goldman-Coutts' art dealer chums were very keen on them.'

When Max looked me in the eye, I realised my statement had surprised him.

'They were art dealers, weren't they?' I asked.

Max put his head on one side but did not reply.

'You must have realised that when you were speaking to them? They were even checking out some of the decorative details of the building as I showed them over to the art studio from the entrance hall. I thought we'd never get here.'

'Well, Jochen—' Max began, then he froze. He must have realised, as I did, that it would be highly unlikely that he would have spoken on first-name terms with German visitors he'd never met before, especially as he was just the school security guard.

'You mean you knew one of them already?'

He coughed.

'Yes, small world, eh?'

I remained silent, hoping to draw him out. My tactic worked.

'When I was a freelance, I knew Jochen Braunschweig.'

A freelance security guard? Could that be a euphemism for a mercenary?

'Paths crossed in Berlin, Vienna, and Vaduz. The others less so. Knew them only briefly in Streslau.'

'Where's Streslau?'

'The capital of Ruritania. Small but perfectly wealthy. Borders Germany and Poland.'

'So is that where you learned to speak German?'

He shuffled his feet, avoiding eye contact. 'Oh, picked up bits here and there. You know. Vienna, Vaduz, Bern.'

'So was Jochen in security too?'

He pointed to his right shoe. 'Oh, look, my lace is undone.' He stooped to tie it in a sturdy double bow. 'Mustn't set a scruffy example to the girls.'

I very much doubted the girls regarded Mr Security as a style icon.

'Hang on, are you telling me all four of those German visitors were not art buyers at all, but security guards? If so, they must be well-paid to shell out a thousand pounds apiece for schoolgirls' art.'

Max stood up slowly and brushed crumbs of pastel crayon off the left knee of his combat trousers.

'If I told you, I'd have to—'

I held up my hand to stop him.

'Then don't tell me, Max. I don't want to compromise anyone's safety, especially my own. I guess their names went down on the sales sheet to make it less obvious how much their boss was spending. I'm just amazed to learn that Mr Goldman-Coutts thought the art he was buying was so valuable that he brought four strong men to protect it as he took it home. But why? They were just the daubings of a schoolgirl.'

Max narrowed his eyes. 'Not the pictures they were guarding. Something else. Can't say more. But trust me, Gemma. You'll know soon enough if all goes according to plan.' He glanced at his watch. 'Just keep all this under your hat, okay? Not a word to anyone. Not even Joe. Sorry, got to go now.'

He tapped the face of his watch.

'When? What plan? Whose plan?' I asked, but he just pressed his lips together and remained silent.

Wondering whether the drawing he'd been poring over when I first entered the studio might hold a clue, I crossed to the far corner of the room to see them for myself. It was a black and white piece in the same style as Hector's book-burning picture.

'Ah, they've missed one!' I cried. 'Do you think we should put it in the school safe in case they want to buy this one too?'

Another thousand pounds would make a big difference to how soon my flat might be made habitable again.

I picked the drawing up carefully by the top corners, wary of damaging such a valuable piece, and turned to show it to Max. But while my back was turned, he'd slipped silently out of the studio. His careful tread was sounding on the spiral staircase, across the courtyard, and by the time I reached the door, he was nowhere in sight.

28

FRIEDA'S LOCKET

I looked back at the picture in my hand and found my eye drawn to the monogram. Recognising it at once, I unfastened the locket from my neck and dropped it gently face upwards onto the table beside the picture, lining it up beside the artist's mark. Apart from the lines of the silver engraving being finer than the pen and ink rendition, they were virtually identical: the same ornate C, topped with a delicate coronet that almost disappeared in the intricate floral border. The only difference was that on the painting's monogram, there was a clear horizontal stroke across the middle of the C, turning it into an E. E for Ehrlich.

I bit back a smile. Frieda wasn't being pretentious in putting a little crown over the monogram she'd supposedly designed for her artwork. She'd just copied the emblem from her mother's locket, which she must have been wearing tucked out of sight under her uniform.

Still, I didn't blame her. If my mum had some kind of heritage that allowed her to use a monogram with a coronet, I'd have been tempted to do the same, especially if my mother had sadly died, as

Frieda's had. It was a touching tribute, and I hoped it helped her grieving process.

At least now I was pretty sure to whom the locket belonged. I was guessing the photo and lock of hair must be Frieda's late mother's. The girl must be devastated by its loss and would be delighted to have it returned. I should lose no time in doing so.

I'd arranged to catch up with Joe in the staffroom straight after the last lesson, but my priority now was to find Frieda and restore her precious locket as soon as possible. I hated to stand Joe up, but I was sure he'd forgive me when I explained the reason later.

I descended the spiral staircase and approached the first sixth-former I saw.

'Sallie, was Frieda Ehrlich in your last lesson, please? I have something belonging to her and I'm keen to give it back to her as soon as possible.'

Sallie thought for a moment.

'No, she told Miss Taylor she was poorly after lunch and she hasn't been to afternoon lessons. Nothing catching, I don't think, so your best bet is to go straight to her room. Though if I were you, I wouldn't enter if you can hear her throwing up or anything like that.'

I headed back to the main building and took the two flights of stairs to the corridors housing the sixth-formers' study bedrooms. I headed there now, the locket clutched tightly in my hand.

How strange Frieda's hair should be so pale when her mother's was as bright as flame, I mused along the way. So pale it was almost colourless, like a polar bear's. And her father's was almost black. The picture in the locket was too small for the colour of her mother's eyes to be detectable, but I wondered whether they were amber like Frieda's. So unusual to be so fair-haired with almost orange eyes. I couldn't remember ever seeing that combination in anyone else. Unless...

Dying your hair was forbidden by school rules, flouted only by Oriana, but if Frieda had bleached hers from flame to white-blonde before joining St Bride's, Hairnet would not have known. Yet Frieda had been at St Bride's long enough for a little regrowth to reveal her natural colour. Was she secretly bleaching the roots in her room when no one was looking? After bedtime, perhaps? And more importantly, why?

Arriving at Frieda's room, I raised my hand ready to knock, then paused to listen for any sounds of her presence. If she really was unwell, she might be asleep, and better not disturbed.

From within came the unmistakeable sound of a radio news broadcast – not the usual listening choice of our pupils, who preferred music stations and streaming services. The newscaster was speaking rapidly in a guttural staccato, as if announcing breaking headlines, but the fireproof door was too thick for me to make out the words. Whatever he was saying, I thought Frieda would find it far more interesting news that I had found her locket. She would not mind me interrupting her programme for that.

I knocked and waited for a reply. A scuffing across the carpeted floor told me that she was coming to open the door to me, rather than just calling, 'Come in'. I heard the key turn in the lock, and when she opened the door just wide enough for me to see her face, a surreptitious glance behind her told me the reason for her caution. McPhee was curled up on her bed, tucked half under the duvet, beside a large hollow that Frieda must have just vacated. For a girl who claimed to despise cats, she was being surprisingly hospitable to Hairnet's.

Even though the curtains were closed, and the room was lit only by a dim bedside lamp, I could tell the girl's face was streaked with tears. I guessed McPhee had done his usual trick of homing in on the person most in need of comforting. I held out the locket in the palm of my hand.

'It's okay, Frieda, I've just come to tell you I've found your locket. It is yours, isn't it?'

She gave a cautious nod.

'Please don't cry. It's perfectly intact, so you can stop worrying now.'

She snatched it from me and hugged it to her chest.

'*Vielen dank*, Miss Lamb. Where did you find it?'

'I found it on the lawn by the lake after lunch. I would have brought it to you sooner, but I had to work out first whose it was.'

She opened the door a little wider, then put her free hand to her throat.

'I had not even realised it had gone. But I am very happy it is not lost. Thank you.'

So, if it wasn't the loss of her locket that was upsetting her, what was the cause of her tears? The girl's pastoral care was her housemistress's responsibility rather than mine, and I planned to find Hazel Taylor as soon as I'd finished with Frieda, but now my eyes had adjusted to the dim light, I noticed her face was flushed, and her breathing fast and ragged. Her shoulders sagged as if she bore the weight of the world. Suddenly, she seemed years older than her fellow sixth-formers.

I did not like to leave her like that without further information.

I glanced at the handbasin in her room, wondering whether she might have been sick in it. But it was covered with a towel, laid out to dry – a dark-blue towel spattered with white flecks. Bleach.

'What is it, Frieda? Has something else happened? I'll fetch Miss Taylor directly, but in the meantime, can I do anything to make it better?'

Frieda turned her head towards the radio. Now there was a lull in our conversation, I realised she was listening to a German language station. I closed my eyes for a moment to try to make out the gist of the news story.

'There has been an uprising in Ruritania,' she said in a low, steady voice, but standing up very straight now. 'The generals have been overthrown. The military coup is over, and the Queen will be restored to her throne – if they can find her. They hope the King Consort and Crown Princess Flavia, who fled the country to an unknown destination, may also return to take their place beside her on the thrones of the House of Elphberg.'

Not having been following the political ups and downs of the little Eastern European state, I wasn't sure at first whether she'd perceive that as good news or bad. But then she threw back her blonde hair and reached both hands behind her neck to fasten the chain on her locket. As the locket settled on her chest, the C monogram – or rather E, as I knew it now to be – gleamed in the light of her desk lamp, and the tiny coronet sparkled as if in celebration.

'I may not know much about Ruritania,' I said slowly, 'but I think I'm beginning to understand why that news is so important to you.'

29

FRIEDA'S REVELATION

'But before we do anything else, we must let Miss Harnett know that McPhee is safe and well,' I instructed.

The girl brightened.

'Ah, but she knows that already. You see, I put a note under her study door last night to say he was safe, but I did not sign my name.'

'He's been with you since yesterday?'

'When I came back here after the art sale and was listening to the news, I began to cry. Then I heard him scratching at my door and I let him in. I was glad of his company, but he is not my cat, so after a little while, I opened the door for him to leave but he would not go. But do not worry, I look after him. I give him a dish of water, and I bring my fish from supper last night and bacon from my breakfast and sausages from lunch. That makes him happy, I think.' Her brow furrowed. 'I hope Miss Harnett will not be angry with me.'

Frieda slipped on her shoes before scooping the black ball of fur into her arms and hugging him tight. The contrast between her pale hair and his dark fur was as stark as the squares of a chessboard.

'She will be very glad to be reunited with him, but also hoping that he has been a comfort to you in your time of need. I think she will forgive you for keeping him from her when she realises your circumstances.'

When we arrived outside Hairnet's study, Frieda lingered a couple of steps behind me while I knocked. At the sound of his mistress's voice telling us to come in, McPhee let out a loud chirrup of greeting and bounded into the room before we had crossed the threshold.

At the sight of him, Hairnet leapt up from her chair so quickly that it rocked and almost fell over before she steadied it with one hand. Then she rushed out from behind her desk to gather McPhee into her arms.

'Frieda has found McPhee for you, Miss Harnett.' I tried to let Frieda off the hook for harbouring him.

'Ah, thank you, my dear. I knew in my heart he would be safe, but I am very pleased to see him all the same. Wherever did you find him?'

Her arms full of purring black cat, Hairnet nodded towards the sofa, and Frieda and I went to sit down.

'He found me, Miss Harnett,' said Frieda. 'He came into my room.'

Hairnet nodded sagely.

'Ah, I thought that was where he was. You see, although you did not sign your note last night, you are the only girl in the school who knows how to write in Germanic script. It is not the disguise you had hoped for.'

Frieda's face fell.

'I am sorry to be so dishonest,' she said. 'But I am now going to tell you the whole truth. First, I must think where to begin.'

Hairnet looked from Frieda to me and back for clues.

'I know you are a political refugee with a passport from the

Dominican Republic, although you have likely never set foot there. I assumed you cannot use the one that would reveal your true nationality to travel for some unspecified reason, but your kind sponsor wished to keep that detail to himself. He seemed an honest man, so I respected his request. We have had Russian girls here before with passports from other countries.'

'Olga has one from the Dominican Republic too, Miss Harnett,' I reminded her.

'But your accent is not Russian,' said Hairnet. 'It's as Germanic as your handwriting.'

She picked Frieda's anonymous note from her desk and passed it to me as evidence. I was astonished to see she'd written the note in the archaic Gothic or blackletter script that was once standard in many European countries, and in German until less than a hundred years ago. I found it hard to read and was grateful it had been discontinued before I studied German at school.

'But you've never used this style in your English essays for me, Frieda.'

She gave a small smile. 'That is because you would not have found it easy to read, Miss Lamb. And because I have not used it in my school work, I thought it would be a good disguise for my anonymous note.' She straightened her back proudly. 'My country is the only one which still uses it for official purposes, so we are all taught to write it well at school. It is not easy. But when we have mastered it, we are allowed to develop our own hand instead in Western style.' She frowned. 'Western script was one of many things the generals wanted to ban. They do not like Western things. That is why they did not like my mother's art or her interest in Western culture. They thought that if the common people knew about Western things, it would threaten their power.'

I could hardly contain my excitement.

'I believe Frieda's original passport is not Russian, like Olga's, nor German, Miss Harnett, but Ruritanian. You know, the little German-speaking state that borders Germany and Poland, where a few months ago there was a coup, ousting the Queen and installing a military dictatorship. The Queen disappeared and was presumed either in prison or worse.' I glanced at Frieda, nervous of reducing her to tears again, but she sat straight and proud, accepting my narrative. 'The King Consort and his daughter, the Princess and heir to the throne, evaded arrest and went on the run, undercover in a sympathetic state, of which there are plenty.'

Hairnet's eyes widened for a moment, then snapped shut in concentration.

'Ah, the troubled Elphberg dynasty, of course. Well, I hope they may all be found safe and well.'

Frieda turned to gaze at me, her eyes conspiratorial. 'But you have worked out where that hiding place is, Miss Lamb, haven't you?'

I gave her a slight nod of complicity.

'Miss Harnett,' I began, rising to my feet. Frieda followed suit. 'May I have the pleasure of introducing you to Princess Flavia Elphberg, heir to the throne of Ruritania.'

Miss Harnett's jaw dropped as she jettisoned McPhee from her lap, leapt to her feet and dropped a low curtsey.

McPhee showed what he thought of that by starting to wash his tail.

'But you are too young to be the missing Princess Flavia?' queried Hairnet. 'And too blonde?' She touched her own greying locks.

Frieda, still standing, drew back her shoulders. 'Madam, I am older than I look, and my current hair colour is from a bottle.' She put her hand to her chest, opened her locket and took a few steps closer to Hairnet. 'If you want to see my real hair colour, it is in here – a little of my hair and my mother's hair twisted together as an emblem of our eternal union.' She looked down at it herself. 'Even I cannot tell which strands are hers and which are mine.'

She held up the locket while Hairnet lifted her spectacles to peer at its contents.

'Well, I never. So how old are you now, Your Highness?'

Only when Frieda had seated herself on the sofa once more did Hairnet fall back into her armchair.

'Madam, I am twenty-five. But my father's head of security thought that once we had escaped across the border, the best place for me to hide was in a place no one would think to look for a woman of a quarter-century: in a school for teenage girls.'

She glanced at her long, white socks and shiny, Mary-Jane shoes. 'Unfortunately, his head of security is not so good at fashion choices for girls.'

My conversation with the sixth-formers from earlier in the term sprang to mind – about the incompatibility of desert boots with biker jackets.

'Would that head of security by any chance be Mr Goldman-Coutts?' I asked.

'Herr Goldman-Kurtz, yes,' she replied, enunciating the German original with exaggerated movement of her lips. 'As you may guess, he is not really my sponsor, but my father's employee. He pays for everything with my father's money from his Swiss bank account.'

'I know your mother's whereabouts are a mystery, but I hope the King Consort is safe, my dear,' said Hairnet.

At the note of concern in her voice, McPhee jumped noiselessly onto Hairnet's lap and began rubbing his chin against her sleeve.

'Only if he never gets behind the wheel of a car,' I replied. 'Frieda, I hope you will forgive my insolence, but your father, Herr Ehrlich, isn't really a poor gardener-cum-chauffeur-cum-PA, is he?

It's been a convincing disguise, but I believe he's actually the King Consort of Ruritania. Isn't that so?'

Frieda smiled for the first time in our conversation.

'Yes. He is not very good at driving because he has had little practice. I am not sure he even has a driving licence. But Kurtz, he thinks a good way to hide a king is as a servant. People would not believe a king would work like a peasant for another person. But my father, he too is smart, and he agrees to do it. During the coup he was safer driving a car in the Cotswolds than if he were riding in his golden carriage in our homeland.'

I couldn't help wondering which side of the road they drove in Ruritania.

Hairnet gazed unseeingly into the distance as this news sank in.

'And so when your father was pretending to be working for Mr Goldman – I mean Mr Kurtz – he was actually being protected by him? No wonder poor Mr Kurtz was a little lost when I asked him to tell the girls on his top tips on running a business. I might as well have asked McPhee.'

McPhee jumped back onto her lap and began treading with his front paws, purring loudly.

'But what about when you were in school?' she queried, stroking his soft ears. 'Herr Kurtz could not protect you then.'

'No, but Herr Security could,' replied Frieda. 'You see, Herr Kurtz knows Herr Security from when they worked in their countries' embassies many years ago. Herr Kurtz trusted your Herr Security. When he was searching for an English girls' school in which to hide me, he asked his network of old colleagues from friendly countries' embassies, and Mr Security recommended St Bride's.'

'He brought in more security forces too, didn't he, as the situation in Ruritania became more intense?' I added. 'Those four men who came to the art exhibition with your father and Herr Kurtz to the art sale, they were also bodyguards, weren't they?' I'd said that almost before I had realised it was the truth. 'They weren't there to bid for paintings or to guard Herr Kurtz's purchases, but to protect the King from danger. Even in the safe haven of St Bride's, under the added protection of Mr Security, the King could not be too careful.'

Frieda nodded eagerly. What a relief it must have been to the girl to be able to speak openly after having to keep so many secrets.

'Yes, they were there for my father's safety.'

I gave a rueful smile.

'I can't believe I didn't realise that at the time. Max thought no one else at the school knew any German, as it's not taught here, and he didn't realise at first that I could understand their conversation. When I heard him refer to you as "*die kleine Prinzessin*", I thought he was being condescending, as if you were some kind of self-important brat. I'm so sorry, Frieda, but I didn't realise at the time that he meant it literally. He was talking about the "little princess" of Ruritania.'

Frieda rolled her eyes.

'I am not so little these days. But Herr Security, he first knew me when I was a very small child, three or four, when he worked in Streslau, our nation's capital. He probably still thinks of me as a little girl. My father is like that too sometimes. He forgets I am an adult now. And to be fair to you, Miss Lamb, I put on the act of a brat when I first arrived at the school. I hope you will understand that I am not like that myself. It was part of my disguise. I thought if I was not nice to teachers and to the girls and even to the good McPhee, they would keep away from me a little. My secret was safer if I was close to no one.'

I was glad to hear that had all been for show.

'You acted the part very well,' I said, hoping she would take that as a compliment. 'But even if no one else detected your pretence, I think McPhee understood that, underneath, the real you was far nicer. You have been very, very brave.'

McPhee chirruped at the sound of his name.

'It was hard to be unkind to such a beautiful cat. Of course, I do not hate cats! Although I do love canaries too. I hope McPhee will forgive me. I hope you will all forgive me for my lies and for my unkindness.'

Hairnet gave her most benevolent smile. 'You were in a very difficult position, my dear, and it was clever of you to think of that tactic. It can't have been easy to flee to a new, strange environment and to be unable to draw on the support of new friends.'

Frieda leaned forward on the sofa.

'I will make it up to you, Madam, when I am back in my home-land. Now that the generals are in prison and our dukes and earls are running the country again, it will be safe for my father and me to return.'

Suddenly, she slumped backwards.

'I just hope it is not too late for my dear mother. I pray they find her alive somewhere. God Save the Queen.'

The phone on Hairnet's desk trilled, and she excused herself to answer it, but didn't take her eyes off Frieda the whole time she was talking.

'Max, yes, I know, but Miss Lamb has beaten you to it. She and Frieda are here with me now and have explained the situation. Yes, yes, I see. Then please report to my study as soon as that is done.'

She replaced the handset and returned to her armchair.

'Mr Security has just asked to see me to explain your circum-stances. I must call in the bursar too. But, my dear, I assume you would now like to be reunited with your father to prepare for your return to Ruritania. Will you now go to stay at Torrid Manor for the rest of your time in England? Mr Security tells me the royal Ruri-tanian plane will collect you from RAF Brize Norton tomorrow.'

'Oh no, please may I stay at St Bride's tonight? Torrid Manor is horrible – so cold and dark and damp, and the toilets are just awful. I like it here at St Bride's. It is almost enough to make me want to be a schoolgirl again.'

Hairnet beamed at the royal approval.

'I'm sure that would be fine, my dear. Perhaps you might ask Miss Taylor to organise a little farewell party for you this evening?'

'Please may I give a treat to my friends? I would like to thank them for making me so welcome at St Bride's. I will never forget their kindness. It has not been easy for me to be a good friend to them when I had to hide who I really was. I hope they will understand now that I have no more secrets. Please may I order a pizza delivery from Tetbury? And maybe someone could fetch me some champagne from Torrid Manor's cellars?'

'For sixth-formers only, of course. For those from whose parents we have prior permission for them to have the occasional glass of wine, and perhaps a bottle or two for the staffroom.' Hairnet glanced at her watch. 'Ask Miss Taylor to make the necessary phone calls from the staffroom. Now, run along to tell your friends your exciting news. I do not usually encourage girls to talk about their titles or privileged positions, but I think in your case I will make an exception. You have much to celebrate.'

'Thank you, I will go and speak to them now.' Frieda got to her feet, then hesitated. 'I just hope that by the time I get back to Ruritania, they will have found my mother so she can celebrate too. I may be twenty-five, but I feel too young to be Queen.'

Hairnet clasped her hands in her lap.

'Take courage if you need it from the precedent set for you by our own dear late Queen.'

Thank you, I will. But I hope it will not be necessary.'

30

MAX'S CONFESSION

I was still chatting to Hairnet, explaining how I'd come to my conclusions about Frieda's true identity, when Max knocked at her study door. As he entered, on Hairnet's invitation, I got up to leave, but Hairnet raised her hand to stop me.

'Max, I think you need to hear how much Gemma has deduced about Frieda's – or, I should say, Princess Flavia's – position. It's all rather marvellous. Such an honour for St Bride's.'

'And I'd like you to fill in a few blanks for me, Max,' I added. 'For a start, how come if Herr Ehrlich—'

'King Rudolf,' Max corrected me.

'How come if Mr Kurtz, as I gather we should call him now, was his bodyguard, King Rudolf drove to St Bride's alone to act as my chauffeur? Surely he'd have been at high risk of kidnap or at least interception by Ruritanian rebels?'

Max gave a slight smile.

'You didn't notice my shadowing you?'

I frowned. 'The road seemed empty, in front and behind us, except when he forced an oncoming vehicle to swerve to avoid us when he was driving on the wrong side of the road.'

Hairnet put her hands over her eyes in horror at our near miss.

'Road was empty, but the car boot was full,' said Max. 'Full of me. I'd have leapt out to defend him at the slightest danger.'

'For me too, I hope,' I added.

'Of course.'

'Then how did you get back to St Bride's before I arrived on my return journey in Oliver's car? It was only decided late in the evening that Oliver would drive me home rather than Herr Ehrlich. Goodness!' My jaw dropped. 'I hope you didn't have to spend the whole evening waiting for us in the car boot.'

Max gave a rare laugh.

'Of course not. Kurtz and I are old friends. He took good care of me. Invited me to wait in the kitchen with the King until you were ready to go. At the last-minute change of plan, the King handed me the key to Kurtz's motorbike, and I sped home ahead of you. When you and Oliver arrived at St Bride's, I'd only just closed the gates behind me. Hid the motorbike behind the hedge.'

'Oriana said she'd seen you talking to him as he sat in the car on the forecourt,' I said. 'None of us realised you knew him.'

'Promised Kurtz to look after the King. Whenever the King came here as chauffeur to Kurtz, I never let him out of my sight.'

Hairnet cleared her throat, looking stern.

'Max,' she began, sounding admonitory. 'I pay you to protect our girls and the St Bride's estate, not to go on jaunts off the premises of an evening as an employee of a foreign state.'

Max looked penitent.

'Very sorry, Miss Harnett. Won't happen again.'

Wanting to stick up for Max, who was responsible for bringing us this new pupil, I seized upon a creative way to divert Hairnet from scolding him.

'But what better recommendation could there be for parents concerned about their daughters' safety than a case study of how St

Bride's successfully sheltered an exiled princess until her country was able to welcome her home? We might even ask permission to display the Ruritanian royal coat of arms on our publicity material, with "by appointment to the Royal Family of Ruritania".'

Hairnet sat up a little straighter. 'Why, yes, I can see that would be rather winning. I can't wait to share that idea with the bursar.'

With perfect timing, there was a knock at the door, and the bursar entered the room. He took a seat at an armchair that was the matching pair to Hairnet's, while she and Max quickly brought him up to speed on Frieda's situation.

When they were ready, I made a further bid to defend Max.

'Besides paying Frieda's school fees, Mr Kurtz spent a huge sum on pictures at the art sale.'

'Indeed,' mused Hairnet. 'I wonder why.'

I thought back to the monogram on the expensive pictures.

'Max, I don't think those were Frieda's own work, were they?'

His eyes darted from me to Hairnet and back again he sighed.

'Suppose I can tell you now. No, they were the work of the Queen. A gifted artist, but the westernised style of her work upset the military. Destroyed the painting she was working on when they arrested her, but the King and Princess smuggled out much of her art. Brought them to school for safekeeping. Hid them in the tunnels, where no one would think to look. Planned to sell on the global art market for many thousands apiece. Many, many thousands.'

'I was convinced those four Germans were art dealers,' I said.

'Ruritanians,' put in Max.

'When I escorted them through the building to the art studio, they kept stopping to look at little details of the carvings and the decorations. Either that or thinking of putting a bid in for the St Bride's estate.'

'Checking for bugs,' said Max. 'Hidden cameras, hidden microphones. Might have been installed by rebel spies. Not that they'd have got past me,' he added proudly.

'But why did they pay the school for them?' asked the bursar. 'Why did you put them in the art exhibition for sale when you could have just sneaked them into your car and driven them back to Torrid Manor at any time? We'd never have known.'

'The king wanted to repay St Bride's for keeping the treasured paintings – and his daughter – safe. Amused him to put a few of his wife's paintings in the sale and buy them back. Plenty more where they came from. What he paid the school was a fraction of what Kurtz will sell them for on the global market. Despite its small size, Ruritania is very rich. Extensive natural resources: gold, emeralds, amber, oil. Punches above its weight. Nothing they couldn't afford.'

'No wonder he was so upset when one of the Queen's pictures was sold for twenty quid before they arrived,' I observed.

'He meant to be first to arrive and have his pick of the exhibition. But took a corner too fast and bam! Straight into a ditch. Took all of six of them to get it back on the road. Lost them precious time.'

'But the Queen...?' I began.

'The Queen is safe,' said Max, raising his arms in the air in an uncharacteristic display of emotion. 'Just before I came to join you here, a newsflash on Ruritania's national radio station revealed that she had been traced to a dungeon in a remote castle, rescued by her supporters, and is now on her way to the royal palace in Streslau.'

'Thank goodness for that!' cried Hairnet. 'Now the celebrations can be unconfined! Sherry all round!'

31

ART FOR ART'S SAKE

'What a good thing Frieda's mother was found safe,' said Hazel Taylor in the staffroom next morning. 'I suppose if her art was potentially so valuable, the rebels might have regarded her as a golden-egg-laying goose. That might have been enough to stay her execution.'

'Do you think her art is really that good, judging by the pictures sold at the art sale?' I asked her.

Hazel shrugged. 'They were competent enough that if one of the girls had produced them, I'd probably have given her an A. But you might say the same of Churchill's watercolours, or King Charles III's. But who's to say what a piece of art is worth in monetary terms? It's whatever one is prepared to pay for it, and its provenance can make all the difference. You only need to check out on eBay the ridiculous sums people will pay for a handkerchief owned by Elvis Presley, or a piece of toast that Harry Styles had taken a bite of, to realise that commerce is for fools. But don't tell the bursar I said that.'

We joined the queue at Old Faithful for our mid-morning caffeine fix.

'What about Frieda? I mean, Flavia – Princess Flavia. Why didn't her pastels fetch as much? Has she not inherited her mother's artistic talent?'

Hazel smiled. 'Not really. But anyone who did fork out twenty quid or so for one of her pieces should be laughing all the way to the bank if they had proof of the artist's identity.'

'Do you think I should tell Hector and Sophie that their picture of burning books is by the Queen of Ruritania?'

'Perhaps you had better ask her.'

Hairnet invited all the staff into her study to say farewell to Flavia over a glass of a crisp Ruritanian white wine that Felicity had found on special offer at Lidl, which with amazing speed had just announced a Ruritanian week to celebrate the restoration of the monarchy. They must have had inside information.

Even though we all knew Flavia was well over the legal age to drink alcohol, it seemed odd to be raising a toast to her.

'So will you continue to experiment with pastels on your return home?' Hazel asked her.

Flavia wrinkled her nose.

'No, I do not have my mother's talent or love for drawing or painting. But my father says her artistic talent has come out in me in a different way. He says I am a natural actress.'

Hazel and I exchanged glances.

'I think we'd agree with that analysis,' I said. 'You certainly had us fooled that you were not pleased to be here – and that you didn't like cats.'

Right on cue, McPhee sidled up to Frieda and rubbed his cheek against her ankles. She stooped to stroke his back for a moment. Then she scooped him up into her arms, kissed the top of his head, and returned her attention to us.

'So, do you think I could be a good actress on the television or perhaps in films? Could a princess become an actress?'

For a moment, her amber eyes wide in her appeal, she looked far younger than her twenty-five years. I wanted to tell her what she wanted to hear.

'I think a girl might do anything she aspires to, if she is sufficiently determined.' I reached out to stroke McPhee's thick ruff of black fur. 'Besides, you have a very fine precedent as your role model – or rather for the other way round, a beautiful actress who became a princess.'

'Really?' Frieda brightened. 'Who was that?'

'Princess Grace of Monaco,' I replied.

32

REWARDS ALL ROUND

'So, Max, you knew the girl's real identity all along, but didn't let on to anybody, not even Hairnet or the bursar?' said Mavis, dropping two brown sugar lumps into her coffee. 'I call that betrayal of St Bride's. You've turned mercenary. How much was Mr Moneybags paying you?'

'Take no notice, Max,' said the bursar.

Max, sharpening pencils with a frighteningly sharp blade of his Swiss Army knife, was unruffled.

'Mavis, and the rest of you,' continued the bursar, 'please note that the only party to have gained financially from this whole escapade is the school, from an unexpected extra pupil, for which we've received a whole term's fee, even though Frieda was with us for less than half a term. Plus, we raised about twenty grand in bonus revenue from the art sale, and this morning we received a handsome donation to our roof fund from a certain royal family, enough to fund the entire repair and redecoration job.'

'Please don't tell me they paid you in Ruritanian florins,' pleaded Oriana. 'You have form in misjudgements with foreign currency, Bursar.'

'They paid in gold bullion,' said the bursar proudly, which shut her up. Ever since he'd discovered we had a princess in our midst – and a princess with a wealthy and generous father – he'd had rather a spring in his step.

'That's wonderful news, Bursar,' I said, feeling more optimistic than I had done all term. 'So what will you do now with the profits from the girls' businesses?'

'It's not only about profits, Gemma,' Felicity reminded me. 'We've been teaching the girls essential skills too.'

'Plus, it's made them more interested in my geography lessons,' said Mavis. 'They all know where Ruritania is now. I'm betting they'll be pestering their parents to take them there on holiday at Easter.'

'Don't forgot what Oliver Galsworthy got out of it too,' I reminded them.

The bursar coughed, about to make a big announcement.

'Miss Harnett has declared that all the girls' profits should be returned to them on condition they reinvest them in their businesses. The girls' art sale, for example, will fund a huge supply of materials for them to produce more work to sell, plus new equipment such as easels and drawing boards. An excellent life lesson for them all in the rewards of hard work and innovation.'

Everyone in the staffroom burst into enthusiastic applause. The bursar, not used to such appreciation, coloured a little and beamed at us all.

A few days after Frieda's departure, Oliver had turned up at school out of the blue, clutching a pile of copies of the latest *Sunday Times*, featuring his exclusive interview with the King Consort and Princess of Ruritania – complete with photos – on how they'd lain low in a derelict Cotswold mansion while awaiting the defeat of the military rebels and the restoration of the monarchy.

'The best scoop of my career!' he had declared proudly.

'The best scoop of your career so far, my dear,' Hairnet had replied as we all gathered around to congratulate him. 'You're far too young to rest on your laurels.'

'I'm proud of you, son,' added the bursar, forgetting for the moment that the staff had not officially been told of their relationship. In any school staffroom, the odd unguarded comment is how rumours start, especially when they're backed up by evidence such as the strong physical resemblance between Oliver and the bursar.

'Hmph, I always knew the chauffeur had more class than that awful Coutts pretender,' said Oriana, breaking away from the crowd around Old Faithful to return to her favourite spot on the window seat. 'Fancy stealing the banking dynasty's name to his own ends, just to sound more English. I couldn't trust him after that.' She gazed across the forecourt and up the drive, as if wondering who might breeze in next to disrupt the school routine.

'What's become of him, anyway?' I asked the bursar. I would have liked the chance to say goodbye to him and to thank him for making me feel so welcome that evening at Torrid Manor. His kind gift of snowdrops had brightened up my temporary flat, where the temperature was so cold, the little flowers had lasted almost as long as if they'd been outdoors.

'He's heading back to Ruritania just as soon as he's packed up their things at Torrid Manor,' said the bursar. 'Turns out he's head of the King's security. A pretty smart one too, if you ask me. That changing places routine with the King, disguising him as his chauffeur, with himself as his boss was genius. They certainly had me fooled.'

Mavis the Merciless turned her attention to Oriana now.

'So if you've changed your mind about him, you've missed your chance.'

I was very fond of Mavis and found her entertaining company, but she did take things too far sometimes. Fortunately, Oriana didn't seem to mind.

'Oh, I've already forgotten about him. But I was wondering whether Rudolf has any eligible brothers at home? Gemma, you were very matey with Frieda. Did she ever mention any dashing uncles to you?'

Really, she was incorrigible.

'King Rudolf to you, Oriana,' said Joe, returning to his favourite armchair. He picked up the *Times Educational Supplement* from the coffee table. I went to perch on the arm of his chair, on the pretext of checking the headlines over his shoulder as I sipped my coffee. He lowered the paper and looked up at me, his face neutral.

'So how about you, Gemma? Has being chauffeured about by a king given you ideas above your station? Has the prospect of spending the Easter holidays in Cornwall with a humble PE teacher lost its appeal?'

I edged as close to him as I dared without breaking Hairnet's rule against PDAs between staff and tried to keep a straight face.

'Well, it may not always be easy dating a fellow teacher,' I said slowly, trying not to think of Oliver. 'But whoever said easiest was best? Life would be so dull if we only ever took the path of least resistance.'

He clinked his coffee cup against mine.

'I'll drink to that,' he grinned.

As it turned out, we all had the chance to give ourselves airs and graces on the last day of term, when a small package appeared in each staff pigeonhole, bearing a Ruritanian stamp and containing a silver medal on a purple ribbon for services to the Ruritanian royal family. But it was McPhee who earned the greatest reward: an emerald encrusted collar, delivered by courier.

The girls didn't go unrewarded either, each receiving a silver brooch in the design of a five-petalled rose, the Ruritanian national flower, and a thank-you card signed by Princess Flavia. Hairnet presented them at the end of term as prizes for their Essential Skills projects, commending everyone for their effort, no matter how much profit each venture had delivered. Hairnet's prize for best business went to the Cakesters in Year 8, who had cannily latched on to the needs of all the other girls to provide catering for their events. All the ingredients had been locally sourced, with lavender buns their runaway bestseller.

'There'll always be room for good cake at St Bride's,' declared Miss Harnett as she presented the Cakesters with their trophy, and everybody cheered.

The name Frieda Ehrlich was stencilled on every tile paid for by the King's donation, committing this little episode to St Bride's School legend for as long as the roof remained intact.

But the best rewards of all were the news headlines, features and photographs that radiated out around the world, all stemming from Oliver's initial scoop, recommending St Bride's as the best British school for girls, by appointment to the royal family of Ruritania.

'Brace yourselves, folks,' said Mavis, as we were clearing our pigeonholes ready for the Easter holidays. 'Who knows what all this publicity might bring to St Bride's next term?'

ACKNOWLEDGMENTS

Firstly, although he's no longer around to read this, I would like to thank Anthony Hope (1863-1933) for creating the fictitious, troubled state of Ruritania in his pacy adventure story, *The Prisoner of Zenda* *(first published 1894)*. The name has since become shorthand in popular culture for a small Germanic state in Eastern Europe. I've also borrowed the names of some of the book's characters as a bit of fun for anyone familiar with the story.

Closer to home, I'd like to thank three author friends for various details: Jean Gill for her insights into French attitudes to garden gnomes, Alison Morton for checking the French and German phrases, and Susan Grossey for advice gleaned through her writing on money-laundering prevention.

Finally, I'm very grateful to my fabulous publisher, Boldwood Books, including my editorial director Emily Ruston, structural editor Christine Modaferri, copy editor Emily Reader, and proof-reader Debra Newhouse, for turning my manuscript into the final version now before you, and the tireless marketing team for telling readers all about it.

MORE FROM DEBBIE YOUNG

We hope you enjoyed reading *Artful Antics at St Bride's*. If you did, please leave a review.

If you'd like to gift a copy, this book is also available as an ebook, paperback, large print, digital audio download and audiobook CD.

Sign up to Debbie Youngs' mailing list for news, competitions and updates on future books.

https://bit.ly/DebbieYoungNews

Why not explore the Sophie Sayers Cozy Mystery series...

ABOUT THE AUTHOR

Debbie Young is the much-loved author of the Sophie Sayers and St Bride's cozy crime mysteries. She lives in a Cotswold village, where she runs the local literary festival, and has worked at Westonbirt School, both of which provide inspiration for her writing.

Visit Debbie's Website: www.authordebbieyoung.com

Poison
& Pens

POISON & PENS IS THE HOME OF
COZY MYSTERIES SO POUR YOURSELF
A CUP OF TEA & GET SLEUTHING!

DISCOVER PAGE-TURNING NOVELS FROM
YOUR FAVOURITE AUTHORS &
MEET NEW FRIENDS

JOIN OUR
FACEBOOK GROUP

BIT.LYPOISONANDPENSFB

SIGN UP TO OUR
NEWSLETTER

BIT.LY/POISONANDPENSNEWS

Boldwood

Boldwood Books is an award-winning fiction publishing company seeking out the best stories from around the world.

Find out more at www.boldwoodbooks.com

Join our reader community for brilliant books, competitions and offers!

Follow us
@BoldwoodBooks
@BookandTonic

Sign up to our weekly deals newsletter

https://bit.ly/BoldwoodBNewsletter

Printed in Great Britain
by Amazon

30628330R00121